While the Distance Widens

Stories by

Elizabeth Herron

🌹

FLOATING ISLAND PUBLICATIONS
POINT REYES STATION
1992

ISBN: 0-912449-42-X

Published by:

Floating Island Publications
P.O. Box 516
Point Reyes Station, CA 94956

"My Wife, He Said" won a Hugh Luke Fiction Award and
was published in *Negative Capability* (Volume XI, No. 2, 1991).
It was also a finalist in the Katherine Anne Porter Prize for fiction.

"Susanna Dancing" was first published in *Amelia*. It was a
PEN Syndicated Fiction Project selection and was the first
story selected for PEN's radio project.

"Fallen Angels" first appeared in *Jazziminds* of New York.

Special thanks to the following people, each of whom gave
something without which these stories might not have been
completed and this book might not have appeared: Nora Riley,
Dianne Romain, Jimalee Plank, Jan Beaulyn, Elizabeth Evans,
Greg Mahrer, Patricia Damery, Barbara Marlin, Michael
Traynor, Douglas Colville, Barbara McCoard, Neil Miller,
Meryl Krause, Will Wells, Cindy Ohama, and Michael Sykes.

The author wishes to acknowledge the support of the Damien
Foundation.

For my brother
Tim

CONTENTS

THE VILLAGE OF
SPEECHLESS UNDERSTANDING

THE VILLAGE OF
SPEECHLESS UNDERSTANDING

Henceforth they went one unto another in silence or speaking a tongue strange to the other so that gradually speech ceased and they relied instead on action to make themselves clear. Thus, they proceeded in a kind of anarchy from which it became possible to trust not the word but the deed. It was necessary then to observe each other more closely to study each other's habits—when one rose and when one turned back the covers, when one ate and when one slept, how one murmured (or did not) to the animals that crept close to the fire for warmth in winter, how another reached for his child's hand (or did not) when thunder rolled across the valley.

Each learned to read the character and moods of the other in this manner, deprived of explanation or argument. Each learned to read the rhythms of the other, as they read the sky for rain, the calls of birds and sighs of insects for ripening berries. Disharmony meant only that one had not studied the signs with proper care, had disregarded the signals by which the other declared his intent, or had perhaps misread a gesture—had seen welcome in the inclination of the head or turn of shoulder which in fact had been a slight turning away, a flicker of sullenness to indicate a need for solitude.

Although there was not speech, still there was song—sweet trilling, low gutteral growls and snarls, and plaintive haunting melodies to evoke the inevitable loss entailed in living. And there were singers, whose task it was to voice the collective estate that they might hear their unity, which could best be reflected in this way; though later a woman drew pictures in the sand at the riverbank, and then more pictures on the clay wall of the hut where they lived.

The wall pictures were more disturbing, since the river could not wash them away, and some feared the power of an unchanging shape. What did she mean by this, they puzzled, for they could not ask her, nor could they ask each other.

When they saw that she who had made the pictures behaved otherwise as always—feeding the children, digging for roots with the other women, braiding her hair in the same long snake-like tail from her head—they forgot that she had seemed for a brief while strange and sat close to her again, as they had before, and she smiled in the usual way, herself forgetting, or forgiving, their previous aversion.

The figures she drew with a stick in the riverbank were recognizable by size and appendage as man, woman, or child. In one such picture, drawn in the damp sand sometime in the morning with the eastern sun warming her back, the woman drew a circle of figures of men and women, as well as a number of smaller figures to represent the village children. Within this circular formation each member of the village could be found, and this seemed at the time particularly numinous, so that again, for awhile, the woman who made pictures was outcast and ate alone and slept apart, though this was arranged in a civilized way with subtle shiftings of the body and slightly averted gazes so that no overt disruption occurred, only when each crawled between the covers, the woman knew to make her bed apart in the little hollow on the far side of the hut, and there she curled up with her blanket.

In this place beyond language, when tongue was for taste and touch and wordless song and the mind was free to cultivate the body's speech, the nuances of breath had many meanings, as the widening or narrowing of the eyes conveyed the sentiments of the heart, and the heart itself was heard to beat in harmony or discord with the heart of the village, as this woman's heart was heard, with some confusion, even distrust, when it lifted and hesitated and her breath grew sharp and short while she drew with her stick and her charcoal the outlines of birds and fish and flowers, the shapes of trees and moon and stars, and even the horned, hooved beasts scarcely seen that sometimes passed on the horizon of the plain beyond the forest.

When she drew these things down by the river, the other women stopped humming the little tune they hummed to call the crayfish out from under the rocks and stood around her in a silent circle. When the woman drew a crayfish, they gasped, but she did not notice. She was busy humming the crayfish song as she drew the down-curving tail.

When she finished the front claws, she stopped, surprised to find the other women watching. She laughed and shrugged her shoulders, and the other women went back to the rocks at the edge of the river. Before they could begin to hum again, they saw the crayfish climbing up out of the water onto the rocks, waving their pale feelers and clicking their heavy claws. The women snatched them up and plopped them into the fish basket and put the lid on.

Of course, no one spoke, but they wondered. What magic was this that one woman humming the crayfish song could bring a half-dozen crayfish all the way out of the water? Was it her humming? Or something else—the picture, perhaps? There were stories of great hummers from the Before Time, but none had hummed entirely alone. So once again, the woman seemed strange. She saw that the others avoided her gaze and that, although they gave her a larger than expected portion of the crayfish that night, still they stood slightly apart from her, no more than an extra span of the hand, but she knew by this that they were not at ease with her. And so again she went to the hollow of the hut to sleep alone.

Perhaps it was the loneliness of her sleep that made her dream, and she began to draw, along with the familiar world of her village, things no one had ever seen. She drew two circles, almost but not quite touching, each with a triangle in its center. She drew a flock of long-necked birds with one bird flying distinctly apart from the others. She drew a woman surrounded by bees, whose head was a hive filled with honey, and while the bees rested in her hair, on her shoulders and her breasts, they did not sting her.

She dreamed a great grey wolf emerged from the thunderclouds and leapt toward her singing the Wolf Song. *Father,* she cried in the dream, though she had never uttered a word before. She dreamed herself surrounded by dark fur, warm and rank with the smell she knew as bear. *Mother,* she sighed, and let herself sink in the thick bed of the bear's body. Waking she wondered what could come from such a lineage.

In another dream she wandered lost in a dark forest till there appeared before her an antlered beast, shaggy about the throat, with long slender legs. Instead of bone, his antlers were flames, so a bright light shone all around him, and he led her out of the wood to a broad plain, to a dawn sky. From these dreams she understood that she was kindred to the creatures of the earth.

All the while she dreamed and drew she continued to dig and braid and hull the seeds, and carry the water, and weave the baskets, and, of course, she hummed. And her humming brought success, so that the village was well fed, and no one went hungry, and the women were fertile and bore strong healthy babies—all but the woman who drew. She slept alone, and no man touched her, and she had no children.

One night she dreamed she sat on the bank of the river to watch the full moon rise. And as she watched, she saw lightning strike the moon and a blackness swim out over the milky dish of the moon's face. She heard a humming, and although the tune was strange, it seemed familiar, and she hummed along as the black shape inside the moon changed in slow undulations. This is my body, the woman thought as she hummed. This is my life, she thought. This is my dream. And when she woke, she hummed and she drew circles inside circles.

The village heard this hum, which had never been heard before. What was she calling now, they wondered? The women worried for her, and the men were afraid. But she knew the humming she heard was for herself, and that she must go forth into the world, where it called her to follow.

By signs and gestures she gave the others to understand this, and so they stood back and allowed her to gather her blanket and her basket to leave, and the women wiped their eyes, and the men also, and before she left, each gave her a small gift—a green pebble, an owl feather, the teeth of a mouse, a sweet cake wrapped in leaves, a squirrel skin, a knife of bone. And so she departed.

All this happened in the Before Time of our lives, in the Dream Time of our waking, in the Dark of our light, and we have forgotten what we knew then in the wordless world. We listen to each other's dreams and stories, listening through the words, longing for the moment of recollection that will transform us.

SUSANNA DANCING

SUSANNA DANCING

I FELL in love with my Uncle Gary when I could barely walk, but the summer of my eleventh year I got a crush on my cousin, Boyd. Well, not really my cousin. He was an uncle, too, but such a young uncle! I think he was eighteen that summer. His girl-friend was Mexican, a sultry girl he rarely brought home to the ranch. One Sunday, though, he brought her to supper.

I watched the way Boyd watched Rita. He could hardly take his eyes off her. I pictured them in the cab of the big pick-up at the end of one of the dirt roads that criss-crossed the countryside between the fields of cotton. I imagined them snuggled together in the dark, kissing. And I thought they must do other things, too, because Boyd didn't come home sometimes all night and I knew he was with Rita.

Rita was lithe and quick and quiet, except when she laughed. She wore a red cotton skirt that Sunday, and her calves below the hem were strong and slender. Her ankles were narrow and delicate. The red skirt swirled and twisted around her as she laughed and darted about the packed brown adobe of the yard. The evening was warm, and I could smell the damp of the fields where the ditches had been full and the section flooded.

Boyd's eyes followed Rita—her dusky skin in sharp contrast to the white cotton peasant blouse she wore pulled off at the shoulders. Her wrists made music with the hoop bracelets that slid together up and down her arms. I watched Rita too, half-jealous and half-bewitched myself by her dark beauty.

Someone turned on the radio to the local country western station, and I swayed to the music, eyes still on Rita, Rita and Boyd. My older uncle, the true love of my heart, leaned down to whisper to me, "Are you going to dance for us?" and straightened up smiling.

The music blared out across the fields twined up with the smell of chicken barbeque, and I began to dance. I step-hopped from one foot to the other and waggled my hips. My uncle clapped his hands and called to me, "Dance, Susanna, dance!" I lifted my arms to the sprinkle of stars that had emerged through the twilight. I breathed deep of the damp air and felt the adobe beneath my bare feet. From the corner of my eye I saw Boyd watching me. I quickened my movements, shaking my shoulders, gliding out into the light that fell through the open door from the new-lit lamps. I whirled and turned, around and around till the faces and trees and house were a smear across the night and the stars all had tails in the sky. I twirled and twirled until abruptly the song ended and the announcer's voice came on. Everything changed. It was over. I stood dizzily still, waiting for the world to settle into place again. There they were, Boyd just turning away, and Rita.

Not long after, the two of them said goodnight and walked out to the old pick-up. I heard the heavy door open and then slam closed. I listened to the engine groan slowly to life, establish a steady rhythm and then fade quickly into the dark as Boyd sped toward town. I stood a long time listening until I heard the cicadas and then my grandmother's voice calling, "Susanna, Susanna!" before I turned and went up the steps.

I never saw Rita again. Mama came and took us to California. Later that summer one of the mustangs, a stallion named Red, reared up and threw himself right over on Boyd—split his pelvis and broke his back. Red did it on purpose. Everybody knew he was mean-spirited and dangerous. Even Papa was no match for him. I wondered what they would do with Red, but last time I saw him he was in the pasture in front of the house. I remember him standing under the cottonwoods, swishing flies with his tail.

Boyd laughed when I asked him about it. "Sure he's here," he said, swinging his chair around and scooting himself out onto the front porch so he could see Red out there. "Sure he's here," he repeated. "Soon's I get outta this chair I'm gonna break his balls. Hear me, Red? I'm gonna break your balls," he shouted, and Red lifted his head and pricked his ears forward.

Mama took us so far away, and I guess I kept traveling in my mind, because I stopped thinking about the cotton and the humid nights. I stopped thinking about Gramma and Papa and Boyd. And then one day I heard my Uncle Gary was dead. He never saw me dancing as I do now, my feet as much a blur as ever the stars and the trees were that night. He never saw me spin like a gyroscope on the single axis of one long leg (for my legs have grown—longer than Rita's were then, and they look even longer *en pointe*). He never saw my arms reach and beckon, animated by all the longing of loss. And yet . . .

How things change. That's what I can't get over. One day, all of a sudden it seems, things are different, and you know you can't go back. I don't think Boyd ever got out of that chair.

Now when I dance, it isn't under the stars and no one calls to me. Even so, sometimes I hear my uncle's voice. It comes from far away and then I hear it like a whisper right beside my ear, almost inside me. "Dance, Susanna, dance!"

WATERCOLOR

WATERCOLOR

CLIMBING the narrow warehouse stairs, I could hear their voices, Jack's low rumble and Annie's voice, higher. Jack's door was partly open. They were over at Annie's. I slid the key into the lock on my door and let myself in. Roy was just inside and came to rub against my leg. He wound his way in and out between my feet while I walked toward the table with the lamp on it and set my books and the bag of groceries down. Just as I switched on the light, I heard Annie's door open, Jack's voice echoing in the hall, "Fuck you!" and Annie yelling, "What is the matter with you? Why are you so impossible? Just get out of here."

I sighed and gave Roy a look. "So it's like that, eh? Don't worry, pardner, it'll be ok." Through the wall I heard Jack rummaging in the kitchen, heard the cork come out of a bottle, then silence. I was putting the groceries away when I heard him cross the outer hall to the stairs. Even his footsteps sounded angry. "There he goes," I said. Roy looked up at me and lifted his front paws alternately one after the other back and forth. "Is that all you can think about? Come on then." I liked the new zip-topped bags. "I suppose you're right," I said, scooping out a bowlful of kibble. I smoothed his fluffy grey coat, while he crunched away. "What's one more crisis? Anyway, it's nice and toasty in here." The radiators were hissing under the long row of windows across the west wall. The windows were dotted with neighborhood lights and distant star-like points of white and orange from further across the city. The warehouse was situated on a hill.

Annie's windows faced north and east. I reminded her often enough that everyone knows a painter needs north light. But Annie always countered that the floor was better in her loft, and everyone knows a dancer has to have a decent floor. It wasn't really the north light I coveted, it was the wall of east windows that gave her morning sun. I envied Annie those windows and the warm swaths of sun she drew the blinds against. As for the floor, it couldn't have mattered less to me. My own floor was splattered with paint that made, according to Jack, a work of art in itself. I had my doubts.

"You should photograph it," he used to say. "It's always changing. It's *Event Art* or something. *Continuous Art.* We should get your friend with the video to come and film it once a week." Jack got excited when he talked about my floor. It bothered him that I was so blase about it. "You should be documenting this," he would rave. "Every week it's a new artifact, this floor. You'd be famous for it. We need to get the archive going, for chrissake, now, not when you're dead and it's too late!"

"Jack, you acted just as excited about the grease spots in Uncle Joe's garage when you were nine years old." I turned to Annie. "He did, Annie. I swear, he was just the same."

Annie stared at us. "You two," she said. "What kind of a family do you come from?"

"Just your ordinary run-of-the-mill lunatics," said Jack. "A bunch of wild Irish."

I thought this was an overstatement. "Not exactly lunatics, Jack."

"Lunatics, the lot of them!" he insisted. "Absolute lunatics. Your father, your brother—. Come on, you can't tell me they aren't crazy. And your mother! God, Mary, she's worse than mine!"

I gave him a dark look. "Never mind about them," I said, and Jack paused.

"Well, you know what I mean," he finished.

"He exaggerates, Annie. You know that by now."

Annie nodded and patted Jack's leg when he plunked himself down beside her. "Yes," she said, "the hooligan." Jack snorted. But he quieted down when Annie touched him.

I liked watching them together—Jack with his wilderness of rumpled shirts and loose jeans, his gritty hands and smudged, half-visible handkerchief, which, so far as I could tell, he used as a rag. In contrast, Annie was neat and graceful, not small, but precise in her movements. Her hands made me think of lace and elegant formal dinners, though there was nothing really formal about Annie. It was her trained awareness of her body, and the fact that she wore small post earrings at a time when heavy dangling conglomerations were the fashion. Annie was lovely. She had strong high cheekbones and a beautiful wide mouth. She always wore dark lipstick, which I never dared to do, because it would draw attention to the scar above my lip. I loved to watch her put her lipstick on. She'd hold the mirror up and put a dark line of lipstick all around her lips. Then she'd fill in with a slightly lighter shade. When she was done, she'd press her lips and rub them together with a fascinating unselfconscious slowness. She had come west from Oberlin to dance with a small avant-garde company. I thought of her arrival like a fresh snowfall, an event unheard of in recorded San Francisco history. She floated into our lives, exotic in her innocence. We loved it that she'd never seen a redwood tree or the ocean, or eaten Thai food, or smoked hash. Jack had seduced her almost immediately. They were, as I saw it, nuts about each other.

Jack was the only one with room in the downstairs part of the building. There he kept his enormous tools for cutting and hammering and shaping metal, and the finest precision tools for small cuts in the steel and copper and brass he used for his complex assemblages. We'd hear him down there, swearing and growling for hours. Then he'd burst upstairs calling us, "Come down here! You've got to see this!"

His daughter sometimes worked with him. Ruby was my second cousin and there was a family resemblance that seemed to startle Annie. It was in our eyes, and something about our chins. At sixteen, Ruby looked more like me than Jack; but she was dark, and her hair was a mass of thick curls. Her mother, Lais, was Nicaraguan. They lived further south, on the edge of the Mission District, but Ruby came by almost every day after school. She'd bring her rap tapes and hang around the studio with Jack, assisting on his projects or working on her own, oblivious to the cold and the hard concrete floor. The only thing she ever complained about was the chemicals Jack used.

"You should stop using that shit," she'd say when he sprayed sealer or paint. "It's going to give you cancer."

"Oh, Ruby . . ."

"If you don't care about yourself, you could at least think of the environment. Or think of me! I'm breathing in here, too, you know."

"Ruby, for chrissake, they don't make anything like this that isn't toxic!"

"They do make non-aerosol dispensers. You should look into it."

"Ok, ok. I'll look into it."

Ruby was a real scrapper, a chip off the old block. She got after me, too, about how I disposed of my turpentine cans. That was before I switched to acrylics. I still missed the old smells of turp and linseed oil, and the paints. Ruby assured me all those beloved odors were only warning me I was being poisoned.

I made a cup of coffee and settled into the overstuffed chair facing the corner of the studio where my current painting was on the easel. I stared at it speculatively. The dark lower area blended roughly into the pale area above it. Without overhead light, the colors were reduced to shades of black, white, and grey, which interested me, because the shapes themselves were easier to appraise.

Roy lept lightly up and balanced on the arm of the chair, waving his tail thoughtfully while he too looked in the direction of the painting. I felt a familiar twinge of sadness, knowing it was almost finished and that once again, as always, it would fall short of the inner vision I trusted and loved and longed to be faithful to. Even when my work was good, it never matched the dream that made me begin it. I didn't take my failure personally. It was the nature of the work never to fully succeed. It was human, I thought, never to create perfection. Maybe not just human but the nature of matter—the material world and its limitations. Such deep thoughts made me sleepy. Still, the slight feeling of sadness was there, right beside the satisfaction, for I did like this painting. Roy did, too. He sat on the arm of the chair contemplating it with me.

"What do you think, Roy?" I sipped my coffee and gave his tail a little tug. From Annie's studio, music began to fill the upstairs rooms. I closed my eyes. Blue music. A wash of color, nearly transparent, then heavy, dark, holding its place, demanding its due. Red and purple. Color swarmed behind my closed lids and I leaned my head against the back of the chair, listening.

It must have been several hours later when Jack came home. I heard him fumbling with the lock on his door for so long I was on the verge of going out to help him when he got the door open and stumbled in. After that I heard him careen around, bumping into things before it got quiet. Passed out, I thought. Annie had gone to bed, though I doubt she could have slept through the racket.

"Are you ok?" I asked, peering over at Annie, who was half hidden in her long wool scarf. We were walking briskly, and when I spoke, my words puffed white in the cold morning air.

"I'm fine." Annie smiled, but I thought I heard a catch in her voice.

"You can't take him seriously," I said. "You have to stand up to him when he's like that. He can be just awful."

"I know. But how can you stand up to someone who's so irrational? He doesn't make any sense. He just wants to fight."

"He's a moody guy." I shrugged. In our family, nobody made sense. We understood each other because we were used to each other. Annie's people must be different, I thought, more normal. "Who knows what it is with him," I said. "What happened this time?"

"I have no idea." Annie's eyes clouded and she started to cry. "Damn," she said.

I put my arm around her waist and hugged her. "Forget him. You're too good for him anyway. He's a jerk. Doesn't know the best thing that's ever happened to him."

"Oh, Mary," Annie pushed the end of her wool scarf across her eyes and sniffed.

"Let's go by the Mexican bakery and get some of those weird cookies," I said, and I grabbed the end of her scarf and dragged her across the street. "Come on," I said, walking backwards ahead of her. I pulled the end of her scarf like it was a leash. "Come on." She had to come, and she couldn't help laughing.

"Look out," she said, warning me. I was about to bang into an overturned trash can, its contents spread over the sidewalk. I sidestepped the McDonald's styrofoam, assorted plastic, newspapers, and aluminum cans, grazing an empty wine bottle that rolled musically across the concrete into the gutter.

"I always wonder if there might be a baby somewhere in the

pile," Annie said. "You see it in the news. I wonder how many they don't find."

Jack must have heard us, because he was waiting at the top of the stairs. He dropped to his knees in the hall. "Forgive me," he said. "I was being an asshole. I'll make it up to you." He smiled, a lopsided dogeared grin, irresistable, I thought. But Annie wasn't going for it.

"You were an asshole," she said, standing a little straighter. "You were a real jerk."

"I know, I know," Jack dropped his head. "But I love you. I can't help it if I'm an asshole sometimes."

"Oh get up," Annie said. "I forgive you." She started to walk past him.

"Come on, baby. Give me another chance. Please."

"But you have to stop acting so mean." Annie was softening.

"I promise, I'll make it up to you. Anything you want, baby." He was sure of himself now. "Give me a hug," he said, and got up from his knees and reached for her.

"I don't know. I'm still mad," Annie said, edging away from him. But he grabbed her.

"Don't be mad, baby. I'll take you to brunch, both of you." He held onto her.

"Let me go," Annie said, pounding his back with her fists. "Let me go, you jerk. You are an asshole. You're still an asshole."

"Hush. Hush," Jack said, holding her. "Shhh."

I shook my head. "You guys," I muttered. "Jeeze Louise, get outta here. You go to brunch, I've got work to do. There's an opening at the University later this afternoon, though, if you'd like to come along. I'd love company."

"I have to work," Annie said. She had a job as a waitress in a snazzy Italian restaurant in North Beach. She wasn't crazy about it, but the tips were good, and her schedule was flexible. "I wish I could. What kind of stuff is it?"

"Paintings. By Abbigail Fox. She's a Sioux woman."

"I'll go," Jack said.

The gallery was crowded, but we got there early enough to see the work. One painting depicted the glowing spirit of White Buffalo Woman against a dark background. A gaunt young Indian man reached for her extended hand from where he sat in the refuse of an urban alley. An empty liquor bottle lay at his side. I wanted to tell Abbigail Fox how much I liked her paintings. She was standing across the gallery in a group of University people, talking with Professor Paul Mahrer.

Jack appeared. "Had enough?"

I hesitated. I'd be able to catch her on Tuesday after her talk. "Ok," I said.

Saturday morning two weeks later, sun flooded Annie's room. She had the curtains back, and she was packing.

"What are you doing," I said, as if it weren't obvious.

Annie's face was pale. She looked like she'd been up all night. Her hair was tangled and stringy, and her eyes were puffy. She had been steadily losing weight over the last few months, and her sweat pants were loose around her hips and thighs.

"I'm going away," she said.

"What do you mean?"

"I don't know. I'm falling apart. I'm going away to think about things."

"Where will you go?"

"Home. To stay with Mom and Dad for awhile."

"How long will you be gone?"

"I'm not sure exactly. Through Christmas anyway. I'll come back after New Year's. Maybe things will be easier with Jack and me. We can make a fresh start."

I sat down on the edge of the bed. "I don't understand," I said. But maybe I did. Hadn't I heard them fighting more and more often?

"Neither do I, that's the trouble. Is it just his way? He's too strong for me. He pushes and pushes and he doesn't listen when I tell him to stop. He's dissatisfied with everything. Is this love, this kind of life? Arguing and making up, arguing and making up. I can't sleep. I can't work. I can't think. What does he want? Does he like it like this?

He thinks I can take it—his moods."

"So you're leaving."

"Yes, I'm leaving." Annie had been gathering her things while she talked, moving quickly, pulling clothes out of drawers and jerking dresses off hangers.

"It's not that I'm a coward, Mary. I hung in. Only now I'm starting to lose it. I feel sick all the time, you know? I can't eat without feeling sick. And I'm getting crazy. I'm getting as crazy as he is. You know what I thought last night? I thought he was going to kill me. I really thought he could do that."

"No," I said. "Jack? He couldn't hurt anybody."

"But he does hurt people. He hurts me. Does it matter that he doesn't mean to? Anyway, sometimes I think he does. It's like he's angry at himself and so he wants to hurt me. I don't know. You see, I'm not making sense anymore. I know he wouldn't hurt me, not really, not deliberately. But sometimes, Mary, I'm afraid. I don't know what he'll do."

"But how can you just go away?"

"I'm getting on a plane this afternoon."

"Does he know?"

"How could he know? He hasn't been home all night. I waited for him. I wanted to talk to him. He could be dead for all I know. Dead in some alley or just dead drunk. How can you stand it? Don't you worry about him?"

"Worry?" I felt vague. "I thought he was here," I said. "I thought he came back last night. I wanted to invite you for breakfast."

"Well, he's not here, and I don't know where he is."

Roy had wandered in and he jumped up on the bed beside me. He climbed into Annie's open suitcase and started to curl up in her clothes. I just watched him, like it had nothing to do with me.

"Oh, Roy," she said, shooing him out. She sat down beside me. "You must hate listening to this," she said. "But I'm tired of trying to be so goddamn cheerful while he uses me for a punching bag."

"Annie, he hasn't ever hit you!"

"No. That's not what I mean."

"Because if he ever hit you . . ." I didn't finish the sentence.

"It's not that I don't love him," she said. "I do. I just can't live like this. I have to go."

I couldn't think of anything more to say. Jack was family. The Hardy's stick together. Blood is thicker than water, Dad always said. "Blood is thicker than water," I said finally.

Annie gave me a despairing look. "I'm not asking you to condemn him. I'm not asking anything anymore. I just want to go away and pull myself together."

When Jack came home and she was gone, he went downstairs and tore the studio apart. It sounded like the garbage truck had gotten inside. After that, I hardly saw him for days. It was nearing the end of the term, and I had so much work to do I was at school till all hours, helping to hang the final show of student work, arranging slides and preparing the papers for exams.

Thanksgiving passed and it was finals week. I was burned out from the grueling intensity of the last month. Then, suddenly it was over. I emerged from the vault-like skylit painting studio and the dark room where I showed my slides. I thought of myself as a mole or a badger coming out of my burrow to see if spring had come. But it hadn't. A cold wind swept the campus, and I put on my coat and gloves to keep from freezing, or I froze, half-dead from the immobility of writing exams and reading papers. Why not just paint? Why not just live? I knew I must be tired to think such dour thoughts. I missed Annie. It scared me to miss someone like that. Almost the way I'd missed Irene, still missed her, though she'd been dead nearly as long as she had lived. "Some things never change," Jack used to say. It was a private joke, not just a joke, much more than that, a secret understanding.

After Irene died, Jack and I had been together constantly. The family didn't seem to notice. Or they just didn't care. Nobody cared much about anything for awhile after Irene died. Jack had held me while I cried in the bathroom after the funeral. We had gone to the Gallaghers' house for the wake and begun drinking. Everyone was drinking—Mom and Dad, Uncle Sean and Aunt Ellen, Uncle Joseph, and Jack's mother, Aunt Lorna, Edna and Katie and Paul and Jack. Someone had even given me a glass half full of whiskey. We were shoulder to shoulder in the dining room late that afternoon, when Uncle Joe started singing.

"Irene goodnight Irene . . ."

"Stop it," I said.

". . . Irene goodnight . . ." they all joined in.

"Shut up," I shouted. Only Jack seemed to hear.

". . . goodnight Irene, goodnight Irene . . ."

I shoved my way toward the kitchen, and darted into the back bathroom. I was throwing up when he found me in there.

"Jesus," he said, and held me while I leaned over the toilet.

". . . goodnight Irene, goodnight Irene, I'll see you in my dreams."

Jack helped me wash my face and rinse my mouth. "What a waste," he said. "What a stupid fucking waste." I knew he meant Irene. I felt dizzy and sick and lost. "Hold on, Mary," he said, "don't let go." Then he kissed me, with all the rage and bewilderment that belonged to both of us. "Mary," he said, over and over, "don't let go."

Later, when I was living in Seattle, he called to say he was getting married. Lais was pregnant. I didn't remember her. "You don't know her," he said. "I met her a couple of months ago." They got married and Ruby was born, and the decade fell away like street lights when it's dark, and you're half asleep riding the trolly home at the end of the day. I came back to the city, and we lived our own lives. Lais and Jack split up the same year I found the warehouse, and before he moved in, Annie arrived on the scene.

Now Annie was gone, and I wasn't sure she would come back. And Jack had been drunk for weeks. There was no point talking to him. Even Ruby had told him she was fed up.

"See you later," she had said, and she hadn't been around after school for days, not even to see if he was sober. "I'm disgusted with him," she said. "He can go fuck himself."

"Your own father?" I was shocked. "You talk like that about him?"

"He's a drunk," Ruby said, "just like Mom always told me."

"No," I said. "He's drinking. He's drinking too much, but he's upset."

"He's a drunk, Auntie. He's an alcoholic, and his life is going to hell. Why do you think Annie left?"

"Annie's coming back. She went home for Christmas. She'll be back after New Year's."

"God, you're as dumb as he is. If Dad can't make a sober phone call, she'll be back for the rest of her stuff, and that's the last we'll see of her." Ruby started to cry. "I'm hanging up now," she said.

"Wait, Ruby—"

"No. I have to go."

"Do you want me to give Jack a message?"

"You still don't get it, do you?"

"What?"

Ruby didn't answer. Finally she blew her nose. "Excuse me," she said. "Look, come for Christmas, ok? Come over here."

I hesitated. "I don't know." I was thinking about Jack and Dad and the rest of them.

"Just an idea," Ruby said. "You're welcome, that's all. Mom said to tell you."

"Ok."

"I'll talk to you later."

"Ok."

I looked around the office. I felt heavy, like I hadn't slept in days, or like I'd been dreaming a long disturbing dream and had just awakened. Why do the people I love have to leave? Annie, Ruby, even Jack might as well be gone. I thought of Irene, who had always been there, just ahead of me, until one day she was dead, her life reduced to the tracks on her arm, and one last pop. It didn't seem possible even now. I saw her as clearly as I had the day we were racing around our new house, with all the cousins hard on each other's heels—Jack and Edna and Paul and Katie, along with Bingo, Grandpa's big Dalmatian. It was the day of Uncle Sean's wedding. Irene and I were wearing the long pale pink dresses Mom had made. We were the flower girls. Bingo was chasing us, and we fairly flew through the kitchen into the laundry room, past the whirring drier, out through the open door onto the steps, Bingo barking wildly, running after us. Irene had already leapt from the porch across the four-foot open space above the still unlandscaped yard, toward the concrete pad, which ran lengthwise across the back of the house beyond the sliding glass doors.

This area was designated the patio, extending into what would one day be the back garden but was as yet only a wide rough field facing northwest. I tumbled out the back door, Bingo behind me. Irene was in the air, as if suspended, her long dress billowing around her, her figure backlit by the setting sun. I thought of heaven, of angels—this is how they must look, golden and glowing, afloat in the light of God's love like the Sisters had said. Bingo slammed into me as he slid off the laundry room linoleum and flew out the door.

I fell without knowing I was falling, hit the dirt without knowing what the darkness was, and the shiny errant edge of a discarded end of roof flashing, invisible in the rough clods of earth, sliced across my face above my lip, so I came up tasting my own blood and saw Irene turn, just at the open sliding glass door, turn and look back because I was screaming. Irene stood like a still in a movie, like one of those photographs taken of the President's wife the day he was shot. I remember that stunned look. Then Irene was running toward me, and she must have been talking too, because her mouth was moving. And Jack was there, leaping off the patio, kicking dirt up where he landed. They were calling my name. "Mary, little Mary," Jack said, when he reached for me.

The desk was piled with papers. The seat of the chair was covered with a stack of prints. Even the lamp shade was cocked at an odd angle. I pulled on my coat and left the office, headed for the bookstore to order the texts for next semester. On the way over I started to feel slightly dizzy. Probably hungry. I couldn't remember when I had last eaten. The sky was clear and though the wind was chilly, I felt the welcome warmth of the sun and stopped, turning to face it. I closed my eyes. Light! Golden light. I felt myself swimming up into that light, into all the colors of the rainbow.

The campus was exceptionally quiet. At the bookstore I checked the new arrivals and considered a book on Bay Area Figurative Art.

But finally, having left my purse in the office, I gave it up and made my way to the back of the store to place my order. Paul Mahrer was there, talking with the manager. Teaching was his life. He was Hungarian and had survived the war in Europe. I knew he had been in one of the camps as a child.

"Hello, Dr. Mahrer," I said. He nodded and held my gaze, not quite placing, but noticing me. His eyes were a stern blue, unmitigated by the slightest hint of humor. In fact, I had never seen him smile. *Tell me about loss,* I wanted to say. *Tell me about forgiveness.* I turned my head in the habitual manner I had with strangers, so the scar above my lip did not show. But something had happened in the look between us, and he chose not to ignore it. He moved close to me to reach for a book on the shelf behind me, and for a moment his hand touched my shoulder, as if in passing, as one might gently touch another in a narrow space or a crowded room. His hand rested briefly on my shoulder, and then he left. I felt a lurch, a kind of physical anguish with his touch, that made me suddenly aware of my loneliness.

He was near the exit, and he followed me. Soon we were walking together.

"Are you finished with your exams?"

"You don't remember me. I'm Mary Hardy. We've met at the union meetings. I teach part-time in the Art Department." He looked surprised, then embarrassed. "I've wanted to thank you for bringing Abbigail Fox to campus," I said. "Her work was very moving. So was her talk." I stopped and we stood a moment. My hair fell across the side of my face, and I felt almost pretty, imagining my hair might glisten in the sun, knowing my mouth was in shadow.

I sensed that he wanted to touch me again, or maybe it was I who wanted to be touched. I could see him lift his hand to brush back my hair, though his hand did not move. He was getting older. In the years since we had first met, he had grown heavier. Today, with his jacket unbuttoned, I saw the white shirt where his belly pushed out. Without choosing the thought, I wondered what he would feel like pressed against me, imagining that soft stomach heaving in above my pelvic bone.

We walked on toward the Art Building. At my office, he hesitated as the door swung open. My paintings glowed on the dark walls inside. The one on the deepest wall reached like the warmth of a fire with its red and gold and orange patches of color. He followed me in, and when I turned, he was very close. For just a second it crossed my mind he had me trapped. Then, just as quickly, I felt a surge of excitement. Maybe I had trapped him. He pushed the door closed. The fire painting took up the whole wall behind me.

"You are on fire." With his low voice and heavy accent, it took me a moment to understand what he had said. By then he had picked up a handful of my hair, lifting it back from my face, above my head, knotting it in his fist and pulling my head slowly back. I tried to turn away, but he tightened his grip on my hair. He looked down at my mouth, then up again and over my head to the painting. He pulled the knot of my hair straight up and then let it go, let it slide through his fingers with a silky rush. "Fire," he repeated, and lowered his hand, still tangled in my hair, to the back of my head to draw me toward him. He held me, and I did not know what to do. I felt small against his bulk, against that stomach that was hard and soft at the same time. I put my hands under his jacket and felt his body through the smooth cotton shirt.

He was big and warm, and lower I could feel his penis like a branch held against his groin, waiting to spring free. He backed me up against the desk and started kissing me, leaving my mouth to put his face in my hair, his lips against my neck, his hands on my shoulders, then down, his palm over my breast, fingers back to my buttons, then in, under the fabric, onto my skin. And then the blur of movement lost its sequence—his head down, mine back, arched away. His mouth on my throat, my chest. His arms around me. His face between my breasts. My hands in his thick white hair, his hands tugging my blouse up, away from the waist of my skirt. And then, he lifted me onto the edge of the desk. "Yes," I said, less a word than a pure exhale. And I opened my knees as he drove them apart, and I reached my hands to his hips to pull him toward me.

It was near dark when we walked to my car, and the wind was cold. *Thank you for strewing the golden leaves,* the line went over and over like a little song in my mind. I wanted to say it to him, but what did it mean? An exaltant little song, like halleluiah, that was all. He himself seemed part of that song, a golden gift. I knew already I would paint this event. At the car I unlocked the door, then turned to him. How soft he looked now. Even in the dusk, his softness was visible, or maybe I felt more than saw it, his whole body seemed more yielding. He pushed me gently against the car. This meeting was a pressing and giving that made us, not two breaking into each other, but one melted together. *Some things never change.*

"How can I leave you?" he spoke softly, his mouth next to my ear.

Don't, I wanted to say. But I didn't. Instead I rubbed my face in his neck, at the open collar of his shirt, and I breathed in—a deep breath of his body. I did not want to be parted from his body, to leave his smell and his warmth.

He leaned back and took my face between his hands and he kissed me once more, and we breathed together. *Con spiritus,* I thought. We had kissed this way before, while he moved inside me. But this was deeper, more calm. I saw behind my closed eyes, spirals of smoke intertwined against white-gold light, against a background that was a mere edge of black.

"Don't say goodbye. I don't want to hear that word." He sounded angry.

I pushed him away just far enough to see his face. "Hello," I said. And I knew I was myself again, that I could get into my car and drive home savoring, remembering, revisioning the colors I had felt in his arms. "Hello, hello!" I was happy, giddy with gladness, holding him until he laughed, and picked me up and spun me around, and the last leaves of autumn swirled at his feet, glowing faintly through the dusk light of the deserted parking lot. I knew then that he was all right too, that he could go home without me.

Jack came in late again. He stood a long time in the hallway before he unlocked his door. Roy sat up on the end of the bed, his ears pricked forward, listening. I was so tired I forgot them both and fell back to sleep. I must have dreamed, although I didn't remember what, but I woke abruptly with my heart beating hard.

The following Monday, I took my Christmas list and charged off to the mall. Several hours later, a bit the worse for wear, I had worked my way to the bottom of the list (catnip) and was heading for the pet shop, when I saw Paul Mahrer going into Macy's. I wove my way through the crowd and followed him. Inside, he had vanished. I passed through notions, accessories, jewelry, glanced into the men's department, passed through shoes and was about to give up, when I saw him at the top of the escalator.

The second floor was a maze of glittering holiday dresses, flocked trees with brilliant gold and pink ornaments, stacks of decorative Christmas gift boxes, and then, off at the far end, in the children's department, I caught sight of him. That white hair was unmistakable. I slowed down. What was I going to say? Would he be glad to see me? I was still some distance, when I realized he was with a child, a little girl about seven, wearing a beautiful cranberry-red coat. I had heard about his nasty divorce; this must be his daughter. I had once had a coat exactly that color.

It seemed as I watched the two of them, I saw something behind him, something like shadows hovering around him. Then, he must have asked her a question, because she nodded, pointed down the aisle, and led him by the hand in that direction.

As soon as I got home, I began a watercolor sketch. I blocked in the red coat first, but the shape of the child grew immediately to a young girl. She was reaching for the hand of a taller man, and behind him, I blocked in several transparent figures, then more. I wanted the sense of generations of men behind this one man, all somehow reaching for the girl. And the girl's red coat began to approximate the shape of a heart, though this was not something you'd notice immediately, with the hem becoming drops of blood. The picture startled me, but I grew more and more certain as I painted it. It was the first remotely figurative work I had done, besides pencil sketches, in some time, and already I wanted to see it big, on canvas. Suddenly I remembered my dream. I had been riding in a car with Abbigail Fox. We were driving over a bridge that was giving way behind us, so there was no way to go back.

It was raining when my friends dropped me off not long after midnight on New Year's Eve. I ran to the warehouse door and waved them away. Their departure was inaudible in the rain. When I got upstairs, I heard Roy meowing from Annie's studio.

"Roy?" I called softly, and listened. "Annie?"

I opened the door. It was dark except for the lights of the city through the rain-streaked windows. Roy rubbed against my feet. "What are you doing in here?" I asked him, whispering, as if it were a secret. "Is Annie back?" I looked across the open floor toward the bed and made out a shape. I slipped my boots off and walked in my stocking feet across that smooth wood floor. "Annie?" I said when I reached the bed.

Jack groaned.

"Jack, is that you?" I sat down. "What are you doing here? Is Annie back?"

"No."

"Oh," I said, and I waited.

"The bed smells like her."

I could barely see him in the dim light. "Jack," we shouldn't be here. Let's go home." He didn't answer. I could smell the whiskey on his breath. "Jack?"

He reached up in the dark and found my face. He drew his fingers slowly down my cheek and lightly traced the scar above my lip.

"It's been a long time," he said, "such a long time, Little Mary."

I closed my eyes. I saw nothing, only blackness. Jack's fingers traced the outline of my lips, then tapped them lightly.

"Knock, knock," he whispered.

I thought to open my mouth, to touch his fingers with my tongue, to hold them between my teeth. But I did not, and his fingers left my lips, slid along my jaw, drawing my hair back behind my ear, tracing its rim, then sliding forward and down the curve of my throat. I stayed absolutely still, while a slow fireworks spread across the black behind my eyes. Jack's fingertips traced the horizontal line of my collarbone, into the little center horseshoe, out along the other side and back to center. He ran the tip of his index finger down my sternum to where the button of my dress stopped him. His hand fell away from me then, and I opened my eyes.

"Mary, help me," he whispered, "now and at the hour of my

death." He wasn't smiling. He was drunk, I knew that.

"I'm not the one you want," I said.

"Please, Mary, I need you now. Wasn't I there when you needed me?"

So, I thought, am I afraid? Of what? That he'll turn on me the way he did on Annie? I took a deep breath. "In your way," I said, and I brought his hand back to my mouth and kissed his palm, finding the rough crevice of his lifeline that ran back toward his wrist like a ragged cut. He rolled, taking me with him, crushing himself against me.

"Am I hurting you?"

"Yes," I said.

"Oh god, I'm sorry." He started to cry, and I held him.

"It's all right, Jack," I said. "It's all right."

FALLING

FALLING

I

IWAS AFRAID Casey would lose her job. She hadn't showed up for work in over a week. I knew she was in trouble when I called every night and there was no answer. Finally I went to her flat on the second floor of a restored Victorian near the hospital.

There were stains going up the stairs—dark splotches against the olive green carpeting. When I saw splashes on the wall, I knew it was blood. I would have turned around, maybe gone for the police or called Leon, my husband, but I guess working at the hospital has steeled my nerves. And in a certain way I wasn't surprised. It was almost as if I had known there would be something like this, as if it were inevitable—even my part in it. So I continued up the stairs, though my heart beat faster and there was a rushing in my ears.

I thought of my children and my husband as I climbed. We're respectable people. We don't suffer. We eat well. We play tennis. We sleep late on Sundays and read the paper in a patch of sun that hangs over the breakfast table. We drink strong steaming coffee—New Orleans blend or Guatemalan, sometimes Vienna Roast.

I thought of these things, watching the reddish smears ascending the white wall, grasping for the safety of my comfortable existence, because I felt the imminence of ruin. If there was blood in Casey's hallway, anything could happen. And so I thought of them—my husband, my children—and my heart beat faster and my breath caught in my throat.

At the top of the stairs I stopped for a minute. The door was unlatched, just the barest crack of light showing the length of it. I pushed it, and it swung open.

She was staring out the window. She was a beautiful woman, slender and dark, with high cheekbones and a mouth like a lush plum. She had long thin fingers that now lay uncharacteristically still in her lap. She sat like a carving, absolutely motionless, as if she had come to the end of a long road and could go no further. Her profile was perfectly framed in the pale square of the window. The west window. There was no place left to go. This is, after all, San Francisco. The land drops from here into the Pacific.

She stared out. She didn't even move to look at me.

"Casey," I said. "Casey, are you all right?" I was standing just inside the door.

At last she turned, slowly, with a great weariness, without surprise, and addressed me. "It flew against the window," she said, "right into the glass."

I knew she meant a bird, though I had no idea when the event had taken place. She might have been sitting there for days.

"It probably only stunned it. They do it all the time at the cafeteria."

"No," she said. "It broke its neck." She looked right at me when she said that, and there was a softness in her face I had never seen before, a great sadness. I realized then how much she had kept hidden behind her humor and her anger.

"It's cold in here," I said.

"Is it?"

I took the shawl off the end of the couch and put it over her shoulders. It was patterned with brightly colored birds.

Casey was afraid of falling. She was afraid of falling down the stairs, she said, afraid of losing her balance and twisting her ankle and falling down into the darkness. Sometimes she woke, out of a dead sleep, clawing for air, for balance, fighting a suffocating obscurity. She said that sometimes her mind seemed to thicken, the thoughts grew so chaotic that the very act of thinking felt like falling, and she wanted more than anything to stop thinking entirely, but she could not. She always held the railing when she walked downstairs. Her long dark fingers closed around the smooth curves of the bannister, choking it with each step. Sometimes, on really bad days, she took off her high heels at the top and descended in her stocking feet, replacing her shoes only when she had reached the bottom of the stairs, just before she opened the heavy door out onto the street. She was afraid of falling, but falling in love is different. Falling in love is like fulfilling destiny.

They had brought him into the hospital in bad shape. We saw them coming, Casey and I. His face was cut or his head, you couldn't tell what. The blood was in his hair, down his cheek, over his ear. A car accident.

They cleaned him up in emergency before they wheeled him into X-ray. That was when she recognized him from the day she'd seen him driving his blue Mercedes with the top down, laughing and flashing his perfect white teeth. Only he wasn't laughing anymore.

She took the handles of the chair and wheeled him to the wall with the grid on it so she could line him up. He turned back toward her, his head lolling.

"Oh God," he said.

"Well, you've still got your teeth." He stared at her uncomprehending. "Face the wall please," she told him.

"No," he said softly.

"No? What do you mean, no?" She already had on her lead apron.

"I can't," he whispered.

"Can't what? Can't face the wall? Come on, I'm just going to take your picture."

"You're going to take an x-ray." There was blood between his teeth, and his lips were so swollen it gave him a lisp. He licked them slowly, as if he were drugged. Of course, he was in shock.

"Look," she said, softening, "it's simple. Turn your head and hold still, and hold your breath for a minute, and it's done. OK?"

He didn't move. His head was half-hanging back over his shoulder with the temporary bandage sliding across his ear.

"Listen, it'll be all right. I promise it won't hurt you." She patted his arm. It was the first time she touched him, and he started to cry. His good eye filled up with tears that dribbled down his cheek. The other eye was already bruising, red and swollen. Casey felt like laughing, not because he was funny, but because she was scared, and she didn't know why. All of a sudden she wasn't sure what was happening.

"Come on, honey," she said. "You'll be OK. Just let me do the pictures. They need to know if your skull is fractured. It'll only take a minute, I promise."

All the while he watched her with that one eye half-closed, the other wide, something happened inside her that she couldn't explain.

"What's your name?" she asked him.

"Joel," he said, blinking up at her.

Casey was with me when she saw him again at the club. He was at the bar when we came in, and he saw her before she saw him. He sat there watching her in the mirror so he didn't have to turn around. He drank whatever it was and ordered another, and he barely took his eyes off Casey.

The first set was almost over when we got there, and on the break my husband came to sit with us. Joel must have gone through some changes over that—a black man coming to our table, sitting down between us, and me a white woman. I'm sure at first he thought Leon was with Casey.

During the second set he ordered another drink, and I got the feeling he was revving his engine to get over our way when Casey caught sight of him.

"Look who's here," she said, nudging me. "Pretty boy." The way she said it, I couldn't tell how she felt about him. She stared at him for a minute and then she got up, slowly, like smoke rising from a fire, and eased her way between the tables over to the bar. I watched her slide up onto the stool next to his, and when he turned to her, she smiled.

He looked nervous.

He was nervous. And yet, he was attractive, I could see it myself, the mixture of vulnerability and apparent honesty, a kind of terrified facing up.

He started laughing and the glass shook in his hand. He was laughing so hard he had to put his drink down on the bar or he was going to spill it all over himself, or all over her—on her sleek white dress and her sweet chocolate skin. He set the glass down, still laughing—foolishly, recklessly. Casey started to laugh, too. She put her arms up so her wrists rested on his shoulders up by his neck, her hands linked behind his head, and she slid off the barstool toward him. Her face was so close to his, he was giddy with it, with her sparkling and the warmth of her body. She was so close. Everything he wanted was right there.

He stood up, too, and tentatively, half-expecting her to push away, he raised his hands to her waist. He wasn't laughing anymore, he was just looking into her eyes. And they stood like that, in the middle of the smoke and the loud music and the conversation, as if they were alone in the room.

There was a dream she had. She says she can't remember when it started. She dreamed of the ice cream shop where the kids in her neighborhood went to buy ice cream cones—fresh peach or French vanilla or chocolate chip. She dreamed she was there again, with her sister Ginny, who has been missing now for two years. They stand at the counter, holding up their money, and the man tells them it is not enough.

"We want chocolate chip," Ginny says boldly, then, remembering, she adds, "please."

But something goes wrong. Something always goes wrong, just when they are about to take the ice cream. Just when he is about to give it to them, he takes it back. "That's not enough," he says. He's yelling at them, ". . . not enough, not enough . . ." and Ginny is crying, and Casey says, "I want it. Give it to me, I want it!" And Ginny is dragging her out onto the hot street with no ice cream like they promised, and the street is on fire, and Casey wants to run back. "Mother fucker!" she yells. "We don't want it anyway. We don't want nothin' you got. Nothin'. We don't want it!"

And she wakes up, hot, the sheets damp. The cool blue light of the street lamp diffused by fog gleams through the window. Joel lies beside her. She is inexplicably angry at him. What is he doing here, his heavy body half-draped across her own? What has he got that she wants? Nothing! She gets up, lights a cigarette and stares down at his still form.

Joel turns in his sleep, his face visible now. She can see his eyes flutter behind the closed lids. He turns his head again, muttering something, and she makes out the pale patch in his hair where they shaved him to stitch his head. He turns again as in his dream the moment comes back to him—his mother's face, cool and smooth as it was that last time, but she is smiling, and her eyes are open.

The impact, the tearing and grinding of the metal, the terrible roar of the crash, the uncontrollable slamming of his body—all this has ceased, and a great silence has swallowed him. And then he sees her, his mother, as she was before they took her and turned her to ash. She stretches out her hand and touches his forehead. And then the sirens come, and out of the dark come the lights.

"Please please please—no!" It is his own voice that wakes him.

The lit end of Casey's cigarette, a red glow like the ambulance lights, grows brighter as she inhales and dull again as the ash thickens over it.

"You OK, honey?" Her voice is disembodied, its source invisible in the night, and then he sees her silhouette as she bends toward him, across the light of the window. She sits down on the side of the bed. He feels her hesitate like a diver on the edge, and hears her sigh, letting go of something. He waits, and finally she leans toward him and brushes his hair back from his face. He closes his eyes in some relief beyond words. He opens them and watches her press her cigarette out and take a sip from the drink on the bedside table. He reaches for her hand. The narrow row of bracelets fall together on her wrist with a small music after which the room seems quieter, more intimate.

"You said please." Her voice is gentle now and nearer. "Did you want something?"

He reaches for her, out of the dream, out of the memory. "You," he says. She laughs softly and slides into bed beside him.

II

"I'm just your backstreet baby, Joel, we both know that, so what are you worried about?" She wanted to stop herself, but the words kept coming. He flushed with anger.

"Shut up!" he whispered. "You don't know what you're saying."

"You just don't want to hear it. You won't admit it. You scared, honey. You think I'm gonna walk up your steps and knock on your front door and ask your daddy if I can come in for cocktails? You think I don't know what's happening? Come on. I grew up on Fillmore Street, right next to Pacific Medical Center—all those clean white doctors. And I said to myself, someday, someday I'm gonna be like them. I'll work there, in that hospital, and I'll be so clean and white I'll be good. You know what I mean, honey? I mean I thought that was the way! That was the way—'cause we all know that's what good is, don't we, good is clean and white." She stopped, out of breath, and waited, but he said nothing.

She felt as if she had kicked him in the groin. Why was she saying these things? What did they really have to do with him? The light of the late afternoon sun hung golden around him. He didn't move. He didn't turn his head away or press his hands together in that gesture of nervousness or boredom or apprehension she had come to know and find so irritating. He did nothing to defend himself, only looked at her, the hurt in his eyes. What did she want him to do?

Her own face felt stiff with resistance. She wanted to laugh, to break the immobility of her mouth, but nothing was funny. Is this what love is, she wondered? All that joy and desire just to suck you in and then it's like everything else, more trouble, more misery? She was angry then. No, it was because he was so fucking insensitive. But already she knew this was not true, no longer believed the words of her attack, the rationale of her cruelty. She glared at him. It had to be his fault somehow.

"My face feels like sheet metal," she said.

He stood to go and leaned heavily toward the door, his weight seemed unsteady, as if his body too surprised him, so that he could not trust it, could not completely inhabit it. She watched him, still frozen, unable to offer even a generous eye.

At the door he turned. She had followed him and stood a step away. "I want you to know, even though I'm going, that I want to stay with you."

He had her then, all over again. She was lost.

"I love you, Joel," she said. Did she mean that? She felt it, but did she mean it? They had their arms around each other and she could feel the release in his body, the breath of anguish he had contained those long lifeless minutes. And she felt her power, felt it like a set of careful daggers, and she knew it was a trap, but she could not escape. Like a sickness, grief possessed her.

What was happening to Casey was happening to me, too. I knew it and Casey didn't. She felt it, I could tell, but she could do nothing. An overwhelming momentum had gathered against what resistance we might have had, an inevitability like gravity. It was a one-way trip down a dead end, but there was no stopping her, no stopping either of us.

By January it was over. Casey hit bottom and the impact set me reeling. To see her defenseless frightened me. To see her vulnerable made me angry. I couldn't sleep. I snapped at the kids. I quarreled with Leon over nothing.

"Leon, something is wrong. She's not herself . . . ," I told him.

"She missed work again, Leon. Leon, for Chrissake stop humming, you're driving me crazy!"

Leon only looked surprised.

And Joel? It hurt me to see him.

There were things she said she didn't remember—days that blurred, hazy moments brought sharply into focus with unpredictable assaults. Moments when something broke or tore open. She could not explain it, why she struck out.

"The Chinese vase," she told me, turning so the light caught her cheek, "it was so beautiful, I wanted it. When it broke, I would have laughed if I hadn't been falling."

Falling. She was falling. He had made her fall. Or she had made him make her fall. "He could kill me," she said. "I could drive him to it." I remember her telling me that. It must have been afterward, because I remember the bruise on the side of her face, the light on it—a deep blue flower pressing out through her smooth dark skin. It shocked me.

We were in the cafeteria at the hospital. She was drinking coffee, the cup on the table in front of her, her hands around it—those long nails, and her lip print, bright against the side of the white mug. I had brought a tuna sandwich, but I couldn't eat.

"Casey, you can't go on with him." I couldn't believe she would, not after that. She looked at me for a minute and shrugged her shoulders. The smoke from her cigarette snaked lazily upward through the afternoon light, curving around her.

"How did it happen?"

"The vase," she said. "It was in his father's house." (Not his house, though he had lived there all his life, "his father's house," she said.) "The vase was in the dining room. We finished breakfast late. We'd slept in. It was Sunday. His father was coming back that night. He was about to take me home. And all of a sudden I got mad. I wanted to hurt him. And then we were arguing."

"What about? What did you say?"

"Oh, I don't know. Something about his mother, I think. I don't remember. Something about—maybe I insulted her. She killed herself, you know."

"I didn't know."

"Yeah. She took an overdose when he was four or five. I probably threw that at him."

I must have looked stunned.

"Well," she said, "none of us is getting out of this alive." She laughed.

Casey was mad. "Damn you, Morgan. You've had everything you wanted all your life. You don't know anything except how to play tennis and the rules for soccer and how to tip a headwaiter. You haven't got any idea what it's like to wear a pair of shoes with soles too thin to keep out the cold of a city street, or what it's like to work your ass off every day with nothing to look forward to but more of the same for the rest of your life if you're lucky. You think a man is stupid if he doesn't talk like you talk. How long could you survive in Harlem? You couldn't even make it in the Fillmore, and the Fillmore is tame, honey, the Fillmore ain't nothin'. You're the worst kind of snob because you don't even know it. You're a goddamn colonialist, you and your prep school education, you and your daddy's bankroll." She was so mad, so mad at all of them, not just him, but the whole thing. "You're a punk, you hear me Morgan, you're a stupid punk kid, you and your privilege!"

She hadn't known she thought these things, but saying them she understood she had wanted to say them for a long time. Something was bursting inside her. A reckless stampede of words spilled off her tongue that she knew she'd regret, but she couldn't stop herself. Suddenly she knew she had always felt this way, from the first time she saw him in the intersection in his blue Mercedes with the top down, laughing—so perfect with his white shirt, the collar open under his Navy V-neck sweater. She had loved him, and she had hated him from that very moment.

She thought she was going to cry, so she pushed out more words. "You bastard!" she screamed. "No wonder your momma wanted out, no wonder . . ."

His hand caught her across the left side of her head and spun her backward into the mahogany table. She heard a high ringing and there was a sharp pain deep in her ear. She heard the ringing and she felt her ribs crack into the edge of the table, saw the table skid against the wall, the vase falling, the room upside down, shards of antique porcelain bounding off the wall and floor like marbles from an overturned Chinese checkerboard. And then she felt a simple sense of sheer relief.

"I never meant to hurt him. I mean, I didn't plan it. I didn't set out to do it. I didn't even want to do it!"

"But you just said—you said you were mad. You were mad and you wanted to hurt him."

"Did I? Did I say that?" She stopped, startled into stillness and silence. And then, as if puzzled, she cocked her head slightly to one side. "Did I?"

"Yes, you did."

She turned her face away and looked down at the grey formica table top, at her hands. She picked nervously at a chip in the polish on her thumbnail, stopped abruptly and looked up at me. "I don't know why."

"Why what?"

"Why I said those things to him. Why I sometimes want to hurt him. Even when he isn't doing anything. When he's lying there asleep!"

"Casey, did you ever have a puppy or a kitten and you just wanted to hug it to death?"

"Out of love, you mean? Come on." She was surly. Anger animated her. There was that snarl in her voice. "Come on, Michele, don't give me that crap. Who's hurt anyway? I'm the one who got slugged, remember?" She turned her face and lifted her chin defiantly. The bruise was proof.

"OK, forget it." I pushed back my chair and started to get up. I was angry myself now and confused. I felt drained. There was nothing left, and she couldn't take what I had to give anyway. I had to get out. Out of this room, away from her, away from this place full of sick suffering people.

"Michele, wait!"

She sounded so alarmed, it caught me, brought me back. Her hands were on the table again, gripping the metal edge.

"Michele," she said. "I'm pregnant."

The last watery sun drowned between the prongs of the skyline, and the greyness of the day fell into me like a long shadow. "Oh, no," I said, and I sat down. For a minute I just stared at her. "Oh, no." It was not so much denial as acknowledgement. I had been waiting for this moment without knowing I was waiting. We sat together heavily, like drunks against the side of a building, as the winter dusk drew in around us.

III

What she's going to say, she thinks, is that her momma was sick and she had to. . . . But her momma wasn't sick. And if she was, what about the telephone? Couldn't she have called? Casey's fingers trembled as she fished in her purse for the money. She took the brown paper bag with the bottle of gin in it and walked out onto Fillmore Street. She couldn't go back to work just yet. Why not tell them the truth? She was the one who was sick. Why not tell them that? Oh yeah, sure. Just call them and say you've got the bad blues, baby. Shit, you start talking like that, you say one word, you'll be cryin' into that phone.

The corner came up suddenly and she rounded it, holding the paper bag close against herself. Her purse swung out and hit the side of the building. Instinctively she put up her hand to steady herself, to keep her balance, to keep from falling. Where was she? Almost there! She didn't remember crossing the street!

Momma. It was Momma. She was the one who was sick. Her momma needed her, that was all. Casey was fine. She was just fine. Nothin' wrong with her. Nothin' wrong now. She was fine. It was all over now and she was just fine.

Casey lit a cigarette and leaned back in her chair. "I should quit smoking," she said, without conviction.

It was getting dark, so I called Leon to tell him what was happening. She didn't say much when I got off the phone, just sat there by the window, smoking her cigarette and staring out into the fog. I was starting to wonder if I should ask, or wait for her to tell me, when she began talking about what had happened.

"I hadn't seen him in over a week. I knew he'd be looking for me. So I just didn't come home. I packed my bag and went to my momma's. He didn't know her or where she lives, and I never told him her phone number, so there wasn't any way he could find me.

"You know how it is—the dead of winter. The city's dark—that mean kind of dark. The wind bites through your coat and freezes your ankles and makes your ears hurt. And on the buses everybody's coughing. And the men are all drinking, you can smell the liquor on their breath. Momma's house is on the south side, so I've been on the street more, and I noticed it—how cold the wind was and how it blew the dirt off the streets, grit in your face. And how the sky's never really clear, and a cold grey dirty dampness hangs over us from dawn till dark.

"I picked up a bottle now and again myself—gin, and me and Momma sat in the kitchen and drank gin and hot water, which is also good for the cramps. I had the cramps pretty bad there for awhile. So we drank that gin and talked, and sometimes we drank that gin and watched the TV.

"And Momma put her shawl over my shoulders, this one, with the birds on it. It's from Jamaica, where she was born. And she even sang to me one night. We drank gin and she sang and I cried, just a little.

"After about a week I felt better, so I came back here. And the next thing that happened, he was on my doorstep, ringing the bell. He was crazy.

"'Where the hell have you been?' he says, pushing in the door, pushing right into my place. 'Just where the hell have you been?'

"I didn't know if I was glad to see him or not. I guess I was scared, so I acted cool and didn't answer and went into the kitchen and poured myself a drink. I had that gin with me like a good friend, and I knew I must of been scared, 'cause when I poured that drink my hand shook.

"He looked mad and I didn't know if I was glad to see him or not. I loved him, but he scared me. I knew he was gonna be madder when he found out what I'd done. So I turned around and I told him.

"You're too late, I said. It was like a slap in the face. It was like I'd thrown the gin in his face.

"'What do you mean?'

"You know what I mean. His face got darker. It got dark like the city was dark, that mean dark.

"'Say it then,' he said slowly. 'Tell me, so I know exactly what you mean.'

"No.

"'Tell me, Casey. What did you do?' He was yelling at me by then.

"What do you think I did? I yelled back.

"You gotta tell me, Casey. I have a right to know.'

"You got no rights, you hear me? It's none of your goddamn business white boy!

"He lunged at me then. I threw the glass at him. I grabbed the bottle off the counter and hit him with it, hard, caught his head—glass and blood and gin everywhere. I was still yelling, but I was crying, too, and I said, You get the hell out of here, Joel Morgan, because we're through, you hear me? I don't want to see your face, so you get the hell out.

"And he went. I shoved him out the door. He was holding his head and bleeding just like he was the day I met him, and I wanted him to go. Go on, I screamed, 'cause he was leaning against the wall, not moving, and I wanted him to go, I wanted him out of my sight.

"He took a step or two down the stairs, and then he looked up at me. I couldn't stand it, I wanted him so bad, so I slammed the door and locked it, and I leaned up against it like he was leaning against the wall outside, I knew it, and I pressed my head against that door as hard as I could to press what was inside of my head out, because I couldn't stand it, I couldn't stand it anymore. And I thought, I wish I had a piece so I could blow us both away, put us out of our misery, because we were like two dumb starving dogs, biting each other. I thought we were so far gone, we might as well finish it.

"I would have done it, but I didn't have a gun. I didn't even have enough aspirin to make myself sleep, and the gin was gone. I didn't know what to do, I felt so raw. I went into the kitchen and I got a knife and I had the idea I would cut my wrists with it. I remember the tile, I could just see the blood going around the tile in little rivers between the squares where it dips down. I could see it, red against the white, filling up the cracks. I could see it splattering the walls and the floor and I dropped the knife and I ran to the door and I got the chain off. I was calling him—Joel, Joel—wait—Oh, sweet Jesus! Because all of a sudden I couldn't stand it, you see? I couldn't stand to see him go."

MY WIFE, HE SAID

MY WIFE, HE SAID

I

NO ONE ELSE seemed to notice. No one else seemed especially interested. At least, no one was interested enough to ask him to explain.

"My wife," he said, and stopped, half-pleading was it? Or apologizing? Or asking us something? "My wife . . ." And he shrugged, smiled slightly, spread his hands and opened them, palms up, as if that explained everything. I waited for him to say more.

"Your wife what?" I wanted to ask, but I was too far away. There were too many people between us, and the conversation had already continued to something else, another meeting, nothing so personal as his wife.

Had he said it again? I heard it over and over. I hear it still, when I'm alone sometimes, in the study let's say, bent over a copy of Landsdowne's first volume with nothing particular on my mind but the tilting forefeather of a California quail. I hear his voice. "My wife," he says, smiling, opening his hands.

She haunted me. I suppose that's the best way to say it—her vague smile and the odd absent way she moved. They both haunted me. Paul, I said to myself, you let people distract you. But then, what is my real work in this world if not people? What else is a writer's business?

I saw her for the first time that night. She came in through the kitchen, passing the door to the room where we met, to climb the stairs. The steps were narrow, and climbing them I imagined, would invite a kind of treachery. She gave one quick glance, her head half-turned, the trace of a smile curving her mouth, a smile as mysterious as his unfinished sentence.

"My wife," he said, as if expecting us to understand.

*

I am alone in my husband's house. My steps muffle in the thick carpet. I carry my coffee cup from room to room. Smoke from my cigarette curls around me. I push through it into the next room. I hear his voice. There are other voices also. The dark figures lean toward me. Their teeth click and they turn their heads away, immobile again. I do not know if they have moved or not. I do not know if they have spoken.

"My wife," he said, as I went upstairs. He spread his hands. "My wife," he said, but he did not finish. He cannot tell them. I am waiting for him to tell them.

She shot him. I read it in the papers. The women merge and separate and merge again in my mind. I catch a moth and let it out the window, careful not to remove the dust from its wings with my fingers. Did I dream it all? Am I dreaming now? The woman in the paper, the woman in my dreams, the other women—the woman who died— what is the difference between a martyr and a victim?

The weapons vary. Sometimes guns. Sometimes sharp pointed things. Things that cut. He had the knife upraised. I knew it was too late. Later it was I who held the blade and he who looked surprised. But it was only another dream.

She must have been the kind of woman who made men angry. She knew her behavior was suspect, her voice too loud, the laughter out of place. This rebellion was not in keeping with her pearls, her afternoon dress, her delicate Italian leather handbag.

She said no. And why shouldn't she? What had they ever done for her? What good had it been, that perfect smile, the gloves, the lace and scarves for her head, all those rosaries? What good had it been to restrain herself, to be so careful, hands clasped in her lap, legs crossed at the ankle. In the end she had been powerless and expendable. Intelligence would be more useful, cunning the better part of it, not beauty, and certainly not good manners.

She shot him, or stabbed him. It was after all a harmless event, merely a nightmare, wasn't it? Not like the one in the news. She said no. What was there to say yes to? The headache. Yes, she had a splitting headache. She was bleeding and she had a headache. There was no one to blame. It was her body.

I had shot him, or stabbed him. It was myself I wounded. My head ached. I bled. I was still bleeding. It disturbs me the way the walls of the house are stained. In the bathroom I stare at a box of Kotex. We do bleed. I was bleeding. I had a headache.

*

I don't know about other writers, but parties require an extroversion I seem to lack. I left the crowded room. Outside, the patio was empty, falling away into darkness at the edge of the garden. I stepped off the brick onto the lawn and wished for a moment that I were barefoot. The grass was thick and my shoes sank into it. Behind me the party murmured and broke into laughter, sighed and swelled, flooded and faded back. From somewhere in the trees at the far side of the grass, an owl hooted. I would have liked to see it. I kept walking. The owl was silent, and then again called out, at the same time I heard a glass break and turned toward the house.

*

My husband, Eduardo, has nothing to do with those stained walls, the blood, the sharp things, the clicking teeth. I told him once that he was innocent. I think he was insulted. And I suppose, after all, that I was wrong. What I meant was that nothing had touched him so deeply as to fundamentally alter his world. His life belonged to him. It was not, as was mine, irretrievable. Of course, I was wrong. His life too was no longer his own. Because of me.

When we married, we moved. But there are certain things you cannot escape. And we are strangers here. Oh, he has met people. He brings them home. I hear their talk. It is full of the unconscious assurance that underlies the character of all the people here, except the poor and the old, who understand about disposability. At the meetings they drink wine. It reminds me of my father and all his well-meant liberalism. He told me not long ago that he had never meant for me to take his thought to action, as if it were possible to hold certain beliefs and do nothing. Otherwise, we do not speak of what happened.

My husband writes. Perhaps it matters. Perhaps not. He has to believe that things can change. In any case, he must do something, or we could not go on. And so he writes. He speaks out. He has his meetings. The other writers come, the poets, the journalists. "My wife," he says, but he does not tell them everything.

The woman was blindfolded, a black kerchief tied around her eyes. Later the soldiers took the blindfold off. They had torn her dress, and she hunched her shoulders forward to protect her breasts, to hide them from the men that were everywhere. Not all the men were in uniform. Among them there was one familiar face.

They took her to an area with half-walls, a convergence of corridors, and she was interrogated. The interrogation was brief. They knew all about her. She knew it was death she faced. Death only after something else, something she saw as she suddenly saw her whole life, from a great distance. And she grew up, she grew wise, she grew old in minutes.

Another woman, with long dark hair, was brought in. Soldiers surrounded the two women and began to poke them with the muzzles of their rifles. Their voices were indistinguishable as they crowded around the women, laughing and jeering.

The woman with the long hair taunted them. She fought them. She twisted in their trap. She would not submit. She wanted them to hurry. She wanted to make them angry so they would hurry. She died late that night. She was conscious for the worst of what they did to her. She did not beg for mercy. She knew better. In death she triumphed. Her pride gave Christina courage.

I lived. I woke from the nightmare. I spoke of it, shaping my words precisely, as if my mouth were not quite under control. I trembled. Goose bumps stood up on my skin. My fiance was from an important family, was that why I was spared? No, not spared, released. These words are not the same. I was not spared. It was too late for that. I belong to my husband now. Because of him I was saved, or did Luis change his mind? I owe my life to one of them. My life, for what it's worth. There are marks on my body. I will never have children.

I do not discuss these things with my husband. He is angry be-
cause of what they did to me. He wishes he could have suffered for me.
In the dark, I remember. I do not blame him, but I do not tell him
everything. There are things he does not know. My eyes have a way of
not seeing. My words can separate from my feelings. There is a wall
inside I could not live without. We live now in another city. Each day I
put myself together again. I do not look in the mirror, except to brush
my hair, apply my lipstick, my eyeshadow. I do not look into my own
eyes. Each day, when I put myself together, I try to remember the eyes
of the other, the woman who died. I try to remember the eyes of the
women on television, the women who smile, who are whole and un-
touched. Each day I put myself together. Again.

*

I stepped off into the dark, into the garden, away from the party.
The owl called and I walked toward it. Behind me there was the sound
of glass shattering.

I turned when I heard the glass break, and I saw a woman in a
light dress fall. A man near her stepped back, his body outlined
against the brilliance of the party. The man reached down, speaking
softly to the woman as he took her arm, pulling her to her feet. I was
too far to hear what he said, but I heard her answer as she jerked away.
"No, not now. Leave me alone," and she stumbled out, off the patio,
into the dark toward me. I had not moved and was not visible from
where I stood beside the roses.

Her heel caught in her hem. She tripped, righted herself, and tot-
tered toward me, like a bird awkwardly dragging a broken wing. In
the dark I could not see her face. The dress continued to wobble
toward me like a lopsided moon.

On the patio, the man stood in silhouette, his legs apart, his
hands hanging at his sides, staring after her. He called her name, and I
thought I recognized Eduardo's voice. "Christina!" He waited, then
turned and stalked into the house.

It seemed suddenly quiet. I stood still, though I felt I should
move, knew I should, had an impulse to flee and saw myself escaping

into the rose garden. I stepped back, but the thorns caught my jacket. I heard the shushing of the grass as she trailed toward me, and then her breath, breaking in soft staccato. Before I could retract myself from the grasp of the roses, she was there in front of me. She sucked in her breath and lifted her face, which shone against the night.

"Don't be frightened," I said, feeling quite ridiculous, stuck as I was in the roses. "I was just walking here, to get away from the noise." I spoke quickly, hoping to reassure her, while I extracted myself.

She looked away, and her hair fell like a curtain across the side of her face. The owl called from the far end of the garden.

"It's a great horned owl," I said, and after a moment she asked, "How can you tell?"

"By the way it calls." I managed to pull away from the thorns and gave the call then. It was perfect. From the farther darkness, the great horned owl answered.

*

I come and go from my husband's house. My house? No, I am a voyager now. I know where I am going. In the garden of my husband's house there are cactus plants. They do not bloom often. Their blooms are always a surprise, so delicate amid the spines. In the house of my husband, there is a room where I paint. Secret paintings. Sometimes I paint, and sometimes I sit by the window, looking out into the garden. My husband does not ask about this room or what I do in it. Sometimes I paint, and sometimes I sit looking out at the cactus.

Sometimes the paintings move. The figures, not sharply outlined, but shades of color so close to the background that they are not at first entirely visible—sometimes these figures stir against the canvas. Their teeth glisten. The faces of these figures are in fact more teeth than anything else, teeth and eyes. The eyes are cold and still, while the jaws twitch and the teeth part, one cannot tell if in a laugh or grimace. Almost imperceptibly the jaws move, the heads turn, and the eyes stare straight at me. It has happened, more than once.

"Christina! Christina!" My husband calls to me. He shakes me hard. My teeth rattle and my eyes roll back. "Christina," he says again loudly, and he slaps my face. I struggle against him, pushing my fists into his chest, jabbing with my elbows. I would scratch his eyes if I could reach them. His eyes—my husband. I collapse against him. "Christina," he murmurs, pressing his lips to my hair.

The room smells of turpentine and paint. Outside, moths flutter around the xerophytic arms, the clever spines of the cactus. In the dark the faintly scented blossoms open slowly, petal by petal, only to close again before dawn.

*

In the other garden, Christina stands beside me, a man she does not know. Her eyes are dark and in the night I cannot see them. Her eyes might hold anything. But in fact they hold at that moment nothing at all. We are frozen in the frame, as she was earlier, climbing the stairs, her husband spreading his hands, his sentence unfinished. "My wife . . ." he said. Her smile is fixed, her sidelong glance, as she is fixed now in a different pose, with me. Her torn hem, heavy with dew trails behind her across the grass. Her eyes are empty, stunned. If I could see them, I would see her blank stare as she gazes unseeing into the dark.

"Shall we go in?" I ask. She does not seem to hear. "Shall we go in?" I repeat. She does not reply. "Christina?" Startled, she looks at me. "That is your name, isn't it?" She nods. "Shall we go in now?" She nods again, slowly, and together we turn to face the glittering house.

A man comes toward us through the crowd. In the lighted room, I see it is indeed Eduardo. I step back as he reaches her side and places his arm around Christina's waist, turning toward me.

"So, you have met my wife."

"Please, Eduardo, it's late, let's go home. I'm tired. My hem is torn."

"Of course, my dear. I'll get your coat," and he releases her.

"No, don't." The words escape, surprisingly.

"Come with me then," he extends his hand to me. "It's been a long day," he says. "I'm sure we'll see you again soon. Good night."

And together they turn, Eduardo and his wife, Christina, leaving the party.

II

The letter had come over a week ago. She recalled the moment, standing in the terracotta tile entry, the sun warming her shoulder. She glanced quickly at each envelope. The mail was usually for her husband. Letters to her were rare—an occasional pale blue aerogram, her father's slender script spidery across its face. This letter was different. Her full name was typed neatly above the address—Christina de Silva de Alvarez—on a plain white envelope. She slid her fingernail under the flap at the corner and lifted the edge.

> Dear Christina,
>
> Yes, I know where you are. I have kept track of you and Eduardo, although it has been ten years. It is urgent that I see you. Please come to the Plaza Gardens, #2409, on September 21st. I will be there. I beg you to come. Until then, I remain yours,
>
> Luis

The sentences of the letter were a series of small explosions in her body. She took note of them—ah, there, and again, and another. Her head began to throb. There was a roar almost like thunder, her knees gave way, and it was dark.

In the other world, the world of darkness, they were waiting for her. She was fighting them, and they were holding her down. How many were they? She could not tell. She felt their hands on her. She heard their voices. She heard their clothing—leather creaking, rough cotton against itself. These sounds tumbled together like rocks in rushing water, over and overlapping. They fell together like the sounds in certain pieces of electronic music, jumbled and distorted. Finally there was the emptiness of wind, as on a desert, and she was alone.

She heard her pulse in her ears, as one does under the change of pressure in a plane, or in a fever. The sun on the tiles made a fuzzy brightness that altered the shapes of things. She fought to focus, marvelling at the same time, from that peculiar distance she had come to know within herself, that the world had become an Impressionist painting.

*

Christina's hand hovers a fraction of an inch from the buzzer. Her arm aches. She wants to run down the green carpeted hallway to the elevator. She imagines it. She sees herself from behind, as he would see her from the doorway, running, catching her heel in the carpet, stumbling just as the elevator doors open. She falls inward as the bullets sink into her back, their impact propelling her forward and down.

The door opens. He stands aside, motioning her in, a handsome man, dark and taller than her husband. He stands aside, bowing his head slightly to acknowledge her.

"Christina, come in, please. I've been waiting for you."

The shock of recognition, like a jolt of electricity, a wave of heat, pours over her, and then a numbness, as abrupt as the termination of a heartbeat. She waits for some feeling to return, some intuition of rightness to guide her. But it is too late. She has come this far.

"Please, come in," he repeats, and she sees beneath his elegant assurance, a trace of uncertainty, a flicker of nervousness that crosses the muscles of his face. She steps into the apartment, and he closes the door quietly after her.

She walks forward into the main room, an expensive neutral room like a thousand other rooms in cities all over the world, and she thinks, "Will I die here?" She turns back, toward the way she has come and looks full into his face then for the first time.

"You are still beautiful," he says.

She feels sick. "Luis, what do you want?"

He searches her face. "You never told him, did you."

"No."

"Why not, Christina?"

She looks away. "What good would it have done? You would have had him killed. Or do you think he would have killed you?" She waits. He has a drink in his hand, a pale amber liquid she thinks might be ginger ale. He swirls the ice in the glass, but says nothing, so she continues. "I've wondered. I've asked myself. He loved you, you know. I wanted to leave him that." She turns and faces the open room. "There was even a time when I couldn't remember. I didn't want to remember. And then, one day he spoke your name. He shared his questions with me. What of Luis, Christina? He never said goodbye. Why did he abandon me? And I remembered everything. I was ashamed. I couldn't tell him."

As she speaks, the memories return: Eduardo and Luis at the cafe, animated, intense, arguing, then laughing, parting with an embrace. And when she joined them, Luis greeting her, reserved, formal, averting his gaze, excusing himself, departing with a wave of his hand, his steps fading, leaving her alone with Eduardo, the two of them reaching for each other, in love. She remembers again the night they took her. She had been on her way home after working in the lab. It was a basic biology course, not like the advanced classes Eduardo and Luis had already finished. They were years ahead of her. Eduardo was interning at the University hospital, Luis a class behind him. And suddenly their lives were rubble. Luis vanished. Eduardo even thought for a while that Luis had been disappeared. But there was word of him, friends had seen him. And besides, of all of them, he was the one whose politics would have protected him.

"You were his friend, Luis, why did you do it?"

"I don't know, Christina. I loved you both. You had each other. I wanted to be part of what you had together."

"Then you succeeded."

"No, Christina. You must understand." He seems almost feverish, his words jostling each other in his rush to speak. "The years since then have been torture for me."

"For you! Torture? Come now, Luis."

"Christina, believe me! I've suffered. It's been a nightmare."

She laughs dryly. "A nightmare? For you?"

"Yes, yes."

In his excitement he takes a step toward her. She backs up involuntarily and feels the plate glass window, cool and unyielding behind her. Twenty-four flights below, cars crawl the narrow streets like crabs between the rocks of a tide pool. Swimmers do laps in a stamp-sized aqua rectangle. From her vantage point she is eye level with the clear pale blue beyond the profile of the city. She looks back at Luis. He wears the kind of glasses that change with the light. Closer to the window they are darker. She sees the window reflected in his lenses. She cannot see his eyes, only a confusion of vertical steel and concrete, double reflections, a patch of sky.

"Stay away from me, Luis."

"Christina, don't be frightened."

"Why did you ask me to come here?"

He does not answer right away. Instead he drops his head and lowers his gaze. She watches the pattern in his lenses change, quickly, kaleidoscopically, catching the shapes of table, chair, the corner of the room, the carpet. He seems about to speak, then takes a step to the side and begins pacing.

"Christina, I knew it was wrong, that I should tell them to release you. I could have said it was a mistake, that you knew nothing. You had ideas, yes, but not information. All these years, I've had this on my conscience. I have no wife, no children. I try to remember what I was thinking. Every night for months I had the same dream. Eduardo and I are at the cafe, arguing. There are empty bottles all over the table. The ashtray is full of cigarette butts, smoke hangs in the air between us. Eduardo seems to be fading away. He leans back in his chair, annoyed with me, trying to escape the smoke and my argument. I can't breathe.

"I speak louder, looking at us, the two of us as we sit there. It seems so stupid, this argument. I speak louder, but I can hardly hear my own voice. It seems Eduardo is leaving, abandoning me, though he has only shifted his weight, leaned back in his chair. I'm sure he's not listening. I speak louder still and gesture to explain. Eduardo interrupts me. 'Calm yourself, my friend!' I'm angry and start to get up

from the table, bottles fall and roll off onto the floor. I hear glass break-
ing, and I wake up." Luis paused and looked at Christina imploringly.
"Eduardo was my friend, Christina, my friend."

"Am I supposed to understand this? He was my friend, too.
What do you think it means to have that damaged? He's my husband,
but is he my friend now?"

"Believe me, Christina, I'm sorry beyond words. Beyond
deeds." He swept his hand out vacantly.

"Luis, listen to me. Do you know what I see at night? Can you
guess? I see your face, your eyes. You watch me, even in my dreams.
When I make love with my husband, you are there! You are always
with us. But only I know who you are. I've thought so many times of
what I would do if I ever saw you again. There's so much I want to say,
and there is nothing to say. Maybe I want to kill you. Maybe I want to
do that."

"You would do me a favor."

"Yes?"

"Yes. If you can't forgive me." He stands before her, rigidly erect
with a mechanical military stiffness.

"Forgive you! How can I? A woman died because of you. You
killed her. Can she forgive you? Can I forgive you for her? How many
others were there? What atonement can you make for them? And
what about my life? What about my family? Children! You dare to
talk to me about children?" She pauses, shakes her head, looks away.
"I can't forgive myself, how can I forgive you?"

"Christina, I'm sorry. As God is my witness, with all my heart,
I'm sorry." His shoulders fall forward and he drops his head.

"You lost your taste for torture too late, Luis." Her voice is cold
with disgust as she turns away from him.

"Don't say that, Christina." His eyes fill with tears. "It's not too
late. Please, I beg you, don't turn away from me. I'm desperate."

She turns back to him, angry now, angry at last. "So, you
threaten me. That's what you want. You want to frighten me. Is that
why you asked me here? What kind of forgiveness is that? All right,
yes I forgive you. I forgive you. Is that all? Is that enough? Can I
simply say the words?" There is such loathing in her voice that he

draws back from her.

"Why did you come Christina, if you hate me so much?"

"I don't know. I wanted to tell you. I wanted to avenge her. I wanted to strike you. Yes, maybe I wanted to kill you. There is nothing I can do to tell you how I really feel, what you have done to us. I wanted to spit in your face."

Luis draws himself up once more before he speaks. "Do it, Christina!"

Her mouth is dry, but she spits what there is at him. The drizzle falls on his glasses. She spits again and sobs. The sound grows, ripping from deep inside her, shoving the core of the wound up and out in a cry that floods the room. Luis sinks to his knees.

She goes to him and begins to beat him as she cries. She uses her purse, swinging it over and over him, the black leather like a dark bird, darting and swooping each blow landing heavily against his back, his head, his shoulders, as she circles. His head is bowed. He does not try to defend himself, but remains kneeling, his arms at his sides.

The clasp on her purse breaks open, and the contents of her bag fly from it, over and around Luis, and across the room, against the walls. A tube of lipstick strikes the glass-topped table. Coins spray and ricochet off the wall. Her handkerchief flutters, drapes itself gently from Luis' shoulder, then drops to the floor as she strikes him again. Her compact hits the leg of the chair, sending out a cloud of fine sweet dust. Cigarettes tumble from her open pack and roll along the carpet. A long pocket knife lands near Luis' knee. He raises his head, and the black bird strikes him full in the face, tearing his glasses away. Blood spurts from his nose.

It is the blood that stops her. Dazed, she stands before him, her hair wild, the side zipper of her skirt twisted across her hip, her jacket torn out under one arm. The purse hangs half-open from her hand. She drops it and stares into Luis' eyes. She is still sobbing. Her arm stiff, she raises her right hand above her shoulder and behind her, holds it there the barest moment and swinging forward with all the strength that remains in her, she slaps his face, knocking his head sideways. He rocks back with it, catches and rights himself. He lifts his hand, as if to touch his face, but does not.

Christina is crying freely now, as a child cries. She wipes her palm against her skirt several times, and again, to rid herself of the touch of him. She steps back. He lets go and sags down onto his heels. The blood runs from his nose down the front of his shirt.

Christina surveys the room as if she has never seen it before. She turns and crosses to the hall. In the bathroom she washes her hands first, then her face. Blood speckles the front of her suit. Cold water, she remembers, and sponges away what she can of it, carefully rinsing the pink stains from the white washcloth afterward. The bathroom reminds her of a hospital. She splashes water against the side of the sink till it too gleams white again. Her eyes travel up her image in the mirror. She buttons her jacket and returns her gaze to the glass. It seems she is seeing herself for the first time in years when she looks at last into her own eyes.

Luis has not moved when she returns, except to take his handkerchief from his pocket and hold it to his nose. Christina walks slowly through the room, picking up her comb, her wallet, her keys.

"Will you tell him now?"

She looks at Luis but does not answer. She is in the hall, almost to the door when she hears him again.

"Tell him, Christina."

*

Eduardo unlocked his car and lifted his overnight bag and briefcase into the trunk. On the horizon, clouds piled in a heap of gold, rose, and lavender. When he pulled off Airport Boulevard into the rush hour traffic on the freeway, it was dusk. He reached for the row of dashboard buttons and pulled on the lights. He checked his watch: six-twenty. He turned on the radio. ". . . continue with the evening news. Police investigating a call from an unidentified woman who reported an alleged member of the right-wing death squad, La Mano Blanca, was operating from an exclusive downtown condominium, found the body of a man identified as Dr. Luis Rojas, the victim of an apparent suicide . . ."

A horn sounded, jolting Eduardo to his senses, and he jerked the wheel, swinging his car sharply back into the center lane. He stared ahead at the endless caravan, the undulating pairs of lights stretching away from him. The red dots blurred and melted together. He blinked again and again, while his hands held the steering wheel as if it were the only solid object in the world.

*

I have often thought about that night and the owl we heard in the garden. In mythology, an owl represents death, cold night, and passivity. It pertains to the realm of the dead sun, that is, of the sun which has set below the horizon and which is crossing the sea of darkness. When we met that night, Christina was wrapped in these things, along with a certain blindness, as if she did not see what was right before her. I believe that if we met again, she would not recognize me.

The last time I saw her, she and Eduardo were walking along the harbor, and I remembered the first time I laid eyes on her, the enigmatic smile she trailed behind her like a scarf as she ascended the stairs. In the Hindu tradition, all winged creatures are symbolic of spiritualization, even the owl, which must then be thought of as one imagines the dark side of the moon or the backside of the left hand.

Eduardo has published a book, and his articles appear with regularity in various reputable political journals. Christina travels with him when he lectures. The book mentions her only once, in the dedication. It says simply, "For my wife."

Why have I told you this story? Because these things happen. Because finally everyone knows they happen, but no one wants to talk about it—these things do not happen to us, not to people like us.

I have thought about the fact that people do unimaginable things to each other. I wanted to understand this, because without understanding the inhumanity remains outside oneself, and we maintain the illusion of our separateness. The healing of the world depends upon our reclamation of connection.

I wrote of Eduardo and Christina and Luis to understand their connection. The story is finished, but the questions remain. I still see

Luis behind dark glasses, or with his eyes glazed in death. He dies with his secret, and I am left with the speculative knowledge I have of my own capacity to inflict pain.

I lift my eyes to the window and the quail are there, scuttling from the brush through the grass. A Steller's jay flits bright against the spring hillside, and I take comfort in the ways of a different world.

FALLEN ANGELS

FALLEN ANGELS

YELLOW—the last remaining ticket to the rollercoaster ride of falling and rising fortune. Yellow—the color of my first two-piece bathing suit when I was sweet sixteen. Yellow the color of a panther's eyes. Yellow the color. Yellow. Yell.

She yelled at him and he caught her by the back of her neck. Don't yell at me, bitch. You yell at me, I'll give you something to yell about, hear me? He shook her, then set her down. Yellow. Yellow the neon sign outside the window. Yellow the neon glow across her face. On off on off. He pushed her and she fell across the bed. On off on off. Yellow across his face.

Any deadend room. A life like an alley, strewn with old newspapers, a drunk against the wall, trash overturned. A room like that. Her yellow hair. Not her real color, but they liked it that way. He liked it that way. Yellow hair and pale skin tinged yellow by the neon. On off on off across her body. Her body across the bed.

He isn't looking at her now. His back is turned. He lights a cigarette and smokes, facing the window. On off on off, color spreads and retreats rhythmically across his features. He exhales and the smoke is alternately visible and then not and then again. He inhales and the top of his cigarette glows. The woman is silent.

They are inside me. They are together but they rarely touch. Most of the time they have nothing to say to each other.

The room was once white, now smoke smudged, aged as if the paint itself harbored the odors of cigarettes and sex. A room like that. A room with doors you don't bother opening. A door to a narrow closet, smelling of must, the wooden bar with five remaining wire hangers, black, bent, slightly rusted. The door to the bathroom— cracked mirror, toilet stained with filth, the dark shower, layers of soap drippings and discolored splashes in the sink, the floor crumbling here and there around the chipped tile. The door out, the third door, is the one to the hall.

Hallway carpet worn to threads along the center and before each door down each side, doors through which occasional voices are heard, occasional arguments, the sound of glass breaking. He himself threw a glass against the wall last week. Now one glass remains on the scratched surface of the blond dresser, the dresser that reminds him of his mother, the house in the valley, the ceramic panther that crouched above the matching blond headboard of the bed. Years ago. The panther had yellow glass eyes that seemed to be watching him whenever he went into that room. Yellow glass eyes that stared accusingly, knew what he was thinking.

When he stood before the low dresser in this room, he remembered standing before the dresser in her room, catching the eyes of the panther on him in the smooth surface of the mirror above the dresser. The panther and his mother's room.

He had thrown the drinking glass against the wall because of her, the woman in this room now, the woman who lived here with him, the woman who at this very moment lay across the bed watching him. He lifted his eyes and met hers in the mirror. She did not speak.

She lies across the bed in the yellow neon. Like she's jaundiced. Might be—shooting up like she does, anything, it doesn't matter what, just so it takes her out of this world. She lies there like she isn't ever going to move again. Night after night in the yellow neon. Running. In her dreams she is running. Not to a place or from a place, just running. But she knows the thing she wants to get away from is inside. In her dreams she runs. Awake she runs standing still. Once you fix it's easy, just wait. It takes a long time to come back. One of these days she won't. It's coming back she doesn't want. Not to this room, what does she care about that? It's coming back to herself she can't stand.

Nights I lie awake watching her. One day I'll be watching and she'll leave without saying goodbye, just as easy as she does it now. Only this time, sometime, she'll go home. I'll watch, and I'll be there when her eyes roll back one last time.

She stares blankly, without seeing the man at the window, her mind on something else, hand pressed against the ratty white tufts of chenile on the bedspread, brushing, brushing, back and forth and back again, smoothing the tufts, her mind slipping back as she stares unseeing. Back and forth, a roar rising and falling in her ears, rising and falling as the room fuzzes out of focus, the roar rising and falling.

She is at the beach house in the top bunk, her sister below her. The sound of the ocean rises and falls around them. Slowly, over and over, she strokes the kitten she has taken to bed with her. Gently, over and over, she smooths the soft fur. Jenny? Her sister's voice. She does not answer. Jenny?

Slowly she runs her hand along the kitten's back, feels the vibration under its ribs. She slips her hand under the kitten's chin and strokes, up and down, up and down, the throat humming back to her. The kitten's purr and the sound of the sea are all around her, rising and falling. Jenny? She continues to stroke the small warm ball of fur snuggled against her.

It is morning when she opens her eyes again. He has drawn the blinds. The chenile spread has slipped, tangled half on the floor. She rolls over to face away from the window. He lies beside her. Jenny, you awake? She closes her eyes. She does not answer.

My mother's room. The sleek ceramic panther with the yellow glass eyes, always watching me. The smell of her, the perfume bottles on the dressing table, scents mingled into an invisible thickening of the air with the powdery smell of lemon and roses, warm and sweet. Close to the smell of her, the smell that rose from her skin, from between her breasts, from her armpits, from her whole body as her nightgown fell away from her when she leaned to kiss me goodnight.

The room is empty, waiting. Such rooms are always waiting— waiting for her. Or maybe I am waiting, always waiting, as I was then, for her to come in, to come home. I stand in her room with my back to the panther. Its glass eyes watch me in the mirror above the glass bottles. I breathe, breathing deeply to find her in the thick sweet air. I look up at myself, small and dark, surprised that I look like the child I am, for I feel old, old and desolate. And then I see its eyes, watching me. It crouches on the headboard of the bed above her satin pillows, lavender satin, smooth. The whole room is waiting for her—the bed, the pillows, the clothes hanging in the closet, the jar of cream on the bedside table. Only the panther is not waiting. The panther is watching me.

She's gone. She left the black ceramic cat here to watch me, to keep me from doing things in her room, to keep me from standing here smelling her smell and remembering.

Maybe I'm going to break the perfume bottles, or tear the bed apart, or go to the closet and rip her clothes off the hangers, scatter them on the floor and stamp them with my feet, cut them up with the scissors!

I walk over to the bed and reach up to the shining panther. I knock it off the headboard. Chunks of china shatter and bounce. I see the white inside under the black glaze. The yellow glass eyes lie separated by an expanse of floor, staring up at me like the eyes of a dead fish. I go first to one, then the other, carefully crushing the glass with the heel of my shoe. It crumbles to a fine chartreuse dust. I remember the sound as I ground my heel into it, that particular crunch of glass as I pressed down.

Summoned—they come out of the dark. Children under oak and apple. The orchard, my sister's red sash, her red plastic headband, hair that platinum blonde of later bleached. Those long lashes, the long legs, iridescent blue plastic shoes, black shorts, a purple leotard with narrow red stripes and the red sash—my sister, nose in a book. My sister.

When we were angels, I wrote, thinking of cotton candy and spun glass and faces like my sister's. Thinking of a kind of innocence—singing at top lung, running wild in the woods, shouting and calling through thin air, spilling milk, upsetting chairs, kissing every doll goodnight three times, no favorites. Red, yellow, blue—books we left behind. Out of the woods she, we—all, into the neon lit street, the darkened doorway, deadend alley, the room we cannot leave. The woman lying nude across the bed, the man facing the window, smoking, exhaling into the yellow neon air, that room where fallen angels wait.

Before we were fallen angels we were good and came home at

dark. At dark, trees reach and branches claw our clothes, our hair, catching off guard our innocence, not of anger or fear, but of the accumulation of something like judgement. When we were angels we loved and hated with clarity. We loved or hated completely, without excuse or mitigating circumstance, one moment to the next, innocent of ambivalence or despair, before we were fallen angels.

WHITE NOISE

WHITE NOISE

I

J HED pushed his chair away from the desk, the movement stirring a small stack of papers which sailed to the floor and settled in a haphazard drift. The throaty voice of Lila's cello drifted down to his study, but he was not listening. Bending slowly, he lifted each page, replacing them in the proper order on his desk.

DECTRON CORPORATION
Transfer Project
material: dense radioactive liquid

He became aware of the cello only when it stopped, and found himself listening, anxiously, till it began again with one of his favorite pieces, the one he referred to privately as Haydn's love song. "I heard you up there today," he would tease, "playing that love song again." And Lila would look startled, almost guilty. He would catch her hand. "Come here," he would say.

Jhed blinked and refocused. Beringer Trucking. He pulled open the drawer and found the file. A fairly routine transport of materials to Disposal Area IV. Personnel? Two: driver and shotgun. Containment covered by Dectron. Sealed cannisters, unmarked as usual. Beringer's standard van. A night run.

He wrote the coded digits across the work sheet, keyed for a printout, double-checked it, and pressed the forward button with the Dectron code number. He placed the work sheets in their respective files mechanically, watching his hands move. He saw the finely shaped fingers, the flexible knuckles, the manicured nails, as if they were not his own. A sudden uneasiness overcame him, and then for a moment it was as if someone had caught him by the throat.

With his mouth open, he gulped for air, closed his eyes, and felt a sweat break out over his body. He opened his eyes to look directly into Lila's face, her photograph on the desk before him. He clung to her eyes as he fought for breath. Lila. He wanted her now. He wanted his hands in her thick hair, his fingers pressing up close to her neck, her warm skull. And then it passed, the dizzying panic passed. He was himself again. He took a deep breath and leaned back in his chair.

In the photograph she was looking toward the camera, just slightly to one side of the lens itself, at the photographer. He had taken the picture on their last vacation at the house up north. It was a color photograph, Lila's face against a background of pink tea roses, the ones that grew wild in back of the house, greeting them every year at the end of the symphony season. He stared into her eyes with the relief that you feel when you remember miraculously where you are, waking up in a strange place.

This is how I imagine it was. Not knowing who you are, as if misplacing yourself, forgetting in that desperate moment precisely where you are; you cannot remember even your name. And what you do know, what you sense with every cell of your body, for just that brief moment, is death. You can taste it in the acrid dust that suddenly fills your mouth so you cannot even scream.

I imagine that the death which was so close to you then—behind the keys of your computer, a fine white powder like chalk that rubbed a dryness onto your fingers as you shuffled the papers on your desk— death, your own imminent death, overtook you. And I imagine you knew only that, to the zero of your bones, to the quick of yourself, beyond who you were.

For is it not death we fear in those moments, in that total terror we feel so profoundly and so fleetingly? Where am I? Who am I? For just a few seconds we do not know. And one day each of us will pass through those few seconds on the way, not to returning, but to a final and complete oblivion, or so we fear. There will come for me, as there has for you, a moment when all I know is that I am not coming back, I have no choice but to relinquish everything.

I imagine you felt that then, just the faintest breath of what was to come, just the breath of a real awareness of what your life had already become. And it was to me you looked for salvation. I had begun to understand and to wither under that burden. I wanted to flower like those pink tea roses in the photograph, to blossom in a disorderly

bramble, wild and unpruned. You know that now. Now you under-
stand everything, even what I do not.

When you were home, your presence pulled at me. There were
times, even from the upstairs, even through closed doors and thick
walls, when I felt your need; and like my cello, I could only sing what
was played upon me. So I sang of your loneliness; your losses were
mine. I was irritated with this interference. I wanted to escape, and
thought of leaving you, not for someone else, but simply to be alone.

That morning, when I heard, over the barely audible hum of the
radio from below, your chair scrape back, heard your footsteps on the
stair, I lay my cello aside and rose to intercept you. I did not want your
physical presence, your meticulous gaze, to take possession of my pri-
vate world. So I walked quickly to meet you at the door, and just as I
reached for the knob, I saw it turn. I darted out my hand to press
against the door, to resist, ever so slightly, so as to assert my presence,
my right to privacy. And I knew, even as I allowed it to open, that this
apparently inconsequential trespass could destroy the balance be-
tween us.

You stood in the doorway, just stood there, staring at me. Your
eyes were wide with an expression I did not know.

"What is it?" I had left my work and this interruption meant I
must abandon it for the day. Angry as I was, your look frightened me,
too.

"What is it?" I asked again.

Still you did not move, but stood with one hand on the knob of the
door and other limp at your side, unaware of your fist crushing a blue
linen napkin from the breakfast table. And then you told me.

An almost imperceptible brightness came to your eyes, and I re-
alized with wonder it must be tears. I wanted to reach out to you, to
comfort you, yet I recognized the gravity of the moment, the delicate
process you were engaged in. Rarely did you allow yourself to be so
exposed. I waited, and did not reach to touch you, out of respect for
you, for the feeling you allowed me to witness, which I did not want to
prematurely comfort.

An important world leader, a political figure had been killed. At first I did not understand. I could not remember what faction of the divided world he represented. The name offered some clues, but I could not recall its precise context. Was it one of the Middle Eastern nations involved in constant border and religious conflicts, related perhaps to the country of your origin? Or could it be African? Areas of North Africa I knew had significant Moslem populations. I could not decide if it was important.

I felt only the power of the moment—you standing in the doorway facing me, my wanting to reach out and wanting to give you room, my own need now forgotten. Beyond you, through the north window, a small glow caught my eye and I stared, equally uncomprehending, at the iridescence of a ruby-throated hummingbird, my mind puzzling over a broken image of bodies falling amid the chaos of gunfire, the smoke and thunder of random explosions, patches of blood punctuating the dull brown of foreign uniforms, soldiers breaking formation to scatter with onlookers in confusion and panic, women rushing toward the platform, children screaming.

It seemed I had taken the picture only a little while earlier, but the foreground, which was of course the intended subject, had blurred, or I have forgotten what it was now, which only goes to show how often our true motives are a mystery even to ourselves. She was in the background of the photograph, looking quite as lovely as ever, with her hair, still red as my own, up in braids and her face lightly freckled, not in the least showing her age. Dad was there too, with his usual superior brown bag lunch. She took such good care of him.

The doctor was waiting, a quizzical look on his face. I must appear as distracted as I felt. It was difficult to focus on the problem, the reason I was there. How could I ask him about this uneasiness, which seemed more an unrest of the heart than of the body itself, though I was having trouble sleeping, and my appetite was completely unpredictable. And I did feel edgy, as if something were about to happen that would change everything. The doctor was waiting.

A detachment had surfaced, dividing me. But that was not why I was here. Why was I here?

When you were seventeen, you had quite a reputation. I was

frightened and equally fascinated when I found you watching me come and go, awkwardly lugging my cello. I was still too thin, and almost blind without my contact lenses. But you saw something you liked, because you kept watching me. You still watched me, only something was happening, something I could not control that threatened to alter everything.

I hesitated. "I don't know why I'm here. I'm fine really. It's just..."

"Lila, I know you don't come to see me when nothing's wrong. What is it?"

"Well, I . . ." Where was my little speech with the list of symptoms? What was the use anyway—what would this man be able to tell me that I didn't already know?

I knew from the way you watched me that you had noticed. It was not the distance itself I felt that disturbed me, but my powerlessness to stop it, and the odd relief that accompanied it. You watched me, not in your old way, not taking delight in me, but carefully, sensing the separation occurring within me, which I could not stop, so that finally my remoteness had permeated even our bed. I was slower to warm to you. A preoccupation seemed to draw me away so that your touch stayed more on the surface of my body and I felt less. I did not want to think about you. I would think instead about my music, the piece I was working on. I could hear it in my head now quite perfectly note for note. I could close my eyes and feel the bow in my hand, feel its sticky resistance which I would draw smoothly across the strings so the sound was full of the feeling Haydn intended. Yes, I could close my eyes and feel the weight of the cello against my legs, comforting as an old friend, while everything was changing.

It disturbed me to find the garden neglected. Though the orchard was blooming and humming with bees, the old trees had not been pruned for years. They were gnarled as the hands of an arthritic, the bark twisted around knotholes and half-rotten branches. As I approached one tree, I saw its trunk covered with the nests of innumerable wrens, which had become parasitic. Was it because the tree was dying? How could such lovely little birds be frightening? Why was I frightened?

A child came out of the house. She looked familiar yet she was no one I knew.

She showed me her teeth. Behind her lower front tooth there was a depression which must have been natural and very slight originally, where a large cavity had formed. Clearly the child would require immediate attention or she would lose the tooth. But none of the damage was visible.

So much neglect everywhere—the overgrown garden and the unpruned trees, the parasitic birds' nests like small knobby sores, the sad child with the rotting tooth. Was it my fault? I felt powerless, hopeless, like the old trees, bravely bearing blossoms, like the child smiling as if nothing were wrong.

Who was it between us? Friends, I was certain, but just who they were, these two people between us in the bed, I didn't know. And what were you doing over there, mumbling in your sleep? As I listened, I became aware of something in your mouth. A small snake you had bitten in half, still wriggled wildly, more wildly than your own tongue as you mumbled. One half of the snake had somehow lost its skin and twisted in your mouth, pink and fleshy like a fat earthworm. The two between us were still sleeping peacefully when suddenly you threw yourself across them and your body sprawled over me, a violent insistent weight. Through my nightgown, I felt you, hard and blindly thrusting as you embraced me. Was it an embrace, or were you pinning me down? I wanted to help you in this sudden lust and began to struggle with the nightgown, but you were trying to kiss me, trying to force the wriggling snake into my mouth. I struggled, but you had the strength of ten, and my screams were smothered beneath you.

We were seated together at the table, overlooking the back garden. Once again I had lost my appetite. You were speaking. And as I sat, listening, looking at you with wide eyes, listening—was I listening? I could not remember later what we were talking about. What I remembered was that as I listened, or sat not listening, but looking as if I were listening, I heard my own thought repeated over and over. There was no way that you could hold me now. I sat listening, or not listening, but looking at you as if I were listening, looking into those clear eyes and all their innocence, the trust of years. Looking into your innocence—innocence of me, of my private thoughts, of the knowledge which was inside me like a hard thing, like some angular shape, some stubborn private certainty beneath my soft facade. It was only a matter of time.

I stared out the window at the rain falling on the lemon trees. The storm came like the breaking of some membrane that had drawn taut over the last weeks, taut as my own skin, as my hold on myself, verging on breaking, the strain finally surfacing in a desire to scream. I wanted to scream. Something insisting on release.

We made love, and it eased me. I felt the tension melt a little, yet I knew it was a temporary solution, knew from my own difficult response that part of me had become inaccessible, not only to you, but to myself.

The symphony season was almost over. Afterward, we had agreed, I would go north for a brief vacation. Brief? I could imagine only going, not so much my actual departure—that moment blurred in my mind—but being away. I could imagine it like a deep breath, an absence of walls, wind over open fields.

The grass in the field was overgrazed, short stubble, pale and bristly, with the dry packed earth showing through. There were no shrubs, only occasional large rocks and a cow here or there, stupidly unconcerned and only vaguely interested in what was going on. I crossed the field angling slightly uphill, walking past several of the cows. From below a large outcropping of rock, a wild pig emerged, black and small, but clearly an adult. As he stood in profile to me, I saw the long dark shaft of skin under his belly that indicated a boar. He turned, lowered his head and eyed me uncertainly, wagging his head as if slightly blind, before he took his first steps toward me. I had an adz in my hands and readied myself to meet him. As he neared, with all my strength I swung the adz. The blows sank clear to the handle just above his shoulders.

I must have flung my weapon several times in a rough semi-circle around his neck before his front legs buckled and he fell to his knees. I couldn't help wondering if this was really necessary. I thought of you, my husband—how you had, with a single shot to the head, felled a wild sow, pulverizing the skull and grey matter which held together in the casing of skin over her head, so that you had no idea the extent of the total and immediate devastation of your bullet until you approached the carcass and began to skin her. My own kill, on the other hand, could hardly have been more brutal, though it had been in self-defense. I was shocked by what I had done and couldn't shake the feeling that somehow I had made a mistake.

I waited for him, sitting alone in the luxury of the downtown office. An odd stillness held me—a peculiar detachment. You were in another city. I was in a building you had never seen and therefore could not imagine. It seemed to me that my thoughts of you were the only thing that connected us. I sat on the rose velveteen cushions of a sectional couch that extended around a gleaming black table on which rested, empty and clean, a circular stainless steel ashtray. Across from me was a black telephone on a brushed-silver steel cylinder end table. There were no magazines on the table, and I was the only one sitting there. The emptiness calmed me, and my anonymity protected me. I waited, as empty and open as the polished surface of the black table. It did not matter how long I sat. Time stretched like an empty bed with cool sheets. Time was a blue room in the light of late afternoon sun through a partly opened window.

The ceiling was high, and very white. The floor was finely filled and smoothly waxed. The rooms were filled with light, alive with work—people moving about, conversations, typewriters audible but out of sight. I was safe there. I sat absolutely still in the midst of this unseen activity.

Halfway across the building, was another sitting area, close to the reception desk, a round glass table, with four chrome-framed leather chairs facing each other, and on the table a large glass bowl filled with several dozen bright yellow mums. All this on a lush oriental carpet whose fibers looked like silk, like the silk carpet hung above the sideboard in my parents' dining room.

Alone, with the wall of windows at my back, the sun making my hand a quiet shadow on the composed curve of my lap, I thought of you. I addressed you as some part of myself, someone inside me who was also always partly a stranger, mysterious behind the ordinary talk across years of days together. You were many miles away.

Earlier I had thought that I wouldn't mind dying. As if it were a way of catching up with myself. And what was it I had thought about separation? About my life, all I had been, standing between us like some topographical map, some long geography—the space between New York and California. And we do not know a country till we travel through it.

I was empty, almost serene, but for the slow draining discomfort which over sheer time comes to be called pain. It quieted me. I accepted the inescapable. Distance was soothing, far less difficult to tolerate than proximity in the absence of intimacy.

I was startled to see my old friend coming toward me. I had almost forgotten why I was there. I rose, a little unsteadily, and he took my hand. "Lila, how good to see you." He leaned down to lightly claim the kiss he knew was his.

They were standing about two-thirds of the way up the hill, the pair of them, the buck slightly above the doe, massive against the silver grey of the October grass at the outer curve of the hill that folded in on the farther side of them, darkening where its shadow met the shadow of the hill beyond. I could see them quite clearly from the road below, and then we must have stopped the car and I could see them telescopically, bigger than life, the rough hairs of their coats, the thickness of his shoulders. I remember thinking there must be fewer of them here because they're better fed than the deer we see up north, which look smaller and thinner this time of year and whose ribs are closer to the surface, striping their bodies with faint curving shadows as they move quietly through the late afternoon light against the steeper slopes of the canyons.

And then I was taking aim, unable to stop myself, though it seemed senseless. I can't remember now which is true, but I recall her suddenly bolting, gathering her body inward for the first thrust and spring that broke the inertia of her immobility and sent her hurtling uphill as if she sensed the moment when I knew I would fire.

Or did she stand stock still and only shudder convulsively and recoil from the mortal shock before she fell, collapsing as if every nerve had given out simultaneously, as irrevocable as the pitch dark when you switch off the light.

Out like a light.

And the pointlessness of it is the full weight of her body, her spirit, on my conscience like a slab.

I remember the road was empty except for our car. There was a desolate feel to the grey curve snaking endlessly through these alien yet familiar hills, the sense that the road came and went to nowhere, that this was all there was, the road and the barren hills, and the carcass of the deer. Was it then that I thought of ritual? Or before? I remember wondering if good intentions would suffice in lieu of the exact symbolic pattern I knew must exist to accompany such an act.

Assassin, with the rifle and the telescopic sight and the calculated decision, I was an assassin. Even the car, moving black and soundless over the empty topography of nightmare had the menacing, ominous aura of injustice and brutality that suggested an underworld of hired guns and sadistic sex—a passionless violence, detached, mechanical and meaningless.

Dressed again we stood beside the bed. It seemed to glow with the imprint of our bodies, as if we had become transparent, luminous. It seemed to float, rising slightly off the floor, hovering like a great grey moth under the streetlight through the veiled window—a light that fell through the curtain onto the terrain of sheets where furrows of shadow gathered loosely in a convergence of curves and unfolded again, slightly off to one side, where we had fallen into brief sleep. We stood some moments without speaking. Then, as of one mind, we turned away, into our separateness. I put on my coat. He took the keys from the table.

What caught my eye was the color, that bright almost neon orange of county road crew clothing and equipment. And the movement, because it turned, rolled over in the wind at the edge of the road as I approached, and I had the eerie sensation of the car propelled not by gasoline, not by my foot on the accelerator, but like the orange blanket, by the wind itself—the two of us caught in the same current, beyond our control, impelled by an irresistible exterior force, brought together at the same time we were torn apart, blown past each other in the autumn wind.

And as I hurtled by, I had the sudden certainty that the blanket was—that it contained—that inside it was—*a small body, the body of a child perhaps four or five years old.* As it turned, rolled over at the side of the road and my car streamed past, I had the distinct impression, I knew, that the child's body was there, wrapped in this bright blanket now slightly dulled by dust and stuck with bits of gravel and dry leaves—*a child, yes. Perhaps still alive!* But my hands were paralyzed, my foot would not leave the accelerator to touch the brake and I drove on, seeing over and over in my mind that particular turn of the blanket, that

peculiar way the blanket snarled into itself or around some shape—
that heavy limpness I could almost feel in my own body, recollecting
how we as children let our bodies roll down the slight incline of the
lawn at the old house, savoring the sensation of limbs left behind and
dragging their own weight, the torso twisted at the waist, its gravity
finally slurring first arms, then legs with delicious slowness into the
turning, the lazy lolling of the body loosely leaning after itself, a car-
cass, the child inside allowing, willing but inert.

A child. The body of a child. Of course not. And so the car sped east,
toward home. I did not want to admit this lost brutalized child into my
world, but it had broken through, and the image clung to me as I
drove into the dawn.

Dew glistened on the sleek maroon hood of your car, metal curves
silvered in morning sun. Sun shadows. Light through green leaves.

I opened the door. The telephone was ringing. My coats had fal-
len, heaped on the floor, the closet gaping. And there was something
else, a certain odd disturbance of the air in the room, peculiar marks
on the carpet, pale sandy tracks, the hint of some intrusion, drawers of
the desk partly open.

My boots were as I had left them, neatly paired, as if stood in.
Black branches broke the liquid square of window, the dark car be-
yond. Steady rush of air from heater. The telephone ringing in the
other room.

I opened the door. The intrusion had been earlier, while I was
away. The house was defenseless without me. The books were turned
over. The coats had collapsed like the empty bodies of bag ladies. The
boots were primly paired witnesses. There was sand, pale and bright
on the blue carpet, helpless evidence dragged in against an alien will.
The window had been closed again, like a mute mouth in careful
denial. There were bits of leaves on the floor beneath it.

I opened the door. The phone was ringing. The white hum of the
heater continued. The light on the window remained obscure.

I tried to stay calm. It was over, after all. Whatever had hap-
pened, it was over now.

"Lila, are you all right?"

"The phone was ringing," I said, speaking quickly into the receiver. "It rang and rang. I thought it was you. I wanted to answer, but the house is so strange. The drawers are open. It was quiet. I could hear the heater. But there was something else, a presence. I can still feel it."

"Listen carefully. Are you listening? Lila?"

"Yes, I'm listening."

"Don't touch anything. Lock the house and leave it. Come to the airport and pick me up. Come now. Don't touch anything, you understand?"

"Yes. Yes, I'm coming."

Leaving, I noticed the marks on the carpet had disappeared. I bent down and saw the finest grains of sand where I had seen the bright patches when I came in. Now I wanted to be out of the house, away from the intrusion of this presence, this intruder, who seemed almost to have come from some darkness within me. I wanted to escape and hurried out, locking the door after me. But the innocence of the house was lost. I looked back at the doorway, the heavy Spanish arch that had for so long protected me, so solid and familiar; and I knew that this safety was gone, that this security was forever broken, that the placid surface of my life was now heaving and swelling against itself, like a stormy sea.

Your car—the gleaming dew was gone, dried by the sun which had abandoned it to the shadow of the trees, leaving only the soft glow of a well-waxed surface.

II

It was your grandfather, the friend of the Shah, you plotted to kill each night as you lay in bed before sleep. Your grandfather, Kalim Hashin, who had humiliated you that day by the edge of the pool in the middle of the party, goading you to jump into the deep water, knowing you had not yet learned to swim. Your grandfather, Kalim Hashin, who called you a dokhtar, a girl, and laughed.

"He even looks like a girl," the old man bellowed, enjoying his joke, leaning down to you, his fat belly and cheeks shaking with laughter. "Are you a dokhtar? Hmm?"

You told me you wanted to kill him then, that was the moment. Rage and shame filled your eyes with tears, but Kalim Hashin only laughed harder, till at last, in a reckless fury, you turned, marched to the edge of the pool by the diving board, and flung yourself in, sinking straight as a stone to the bottom.

It was your father who rescued you and your mother who swept you away to the house, weeping as she carried you up the stairs. How amazed you were that she could lift you and carry you all the way up and then down the long hall to her private room, a world you entered only rarely and only by invitation, a room with pink flowered wallpaper.

Every night, you told me, for thirteen years, you plotted revenge. In the beginning you thought you would blow him to bits, watch his body disintegrate in a shower of gore, his terrible smile obliterated forever.

By the time you reached puberty, with this secret anger unabated, you had refined your fantasy. Firearms had replaced explosives as your chosen weapon. Before you left prep school, you had become an expert, favoring particularly the semi-automatic pistol because of the accuracy inherent in its design. And though it was clear to you by then that you could not take your grandfather's life, still you felt cheated by Kalim Hashin's abrupt death, just two days before your seventeenth birthday, a death that left you breathless as a sail gone limp, becalmed on the waters of your rage.

Your depression, interpreted by the family as grief, stayed with you a full year. You were able to shake it only intermittently through the passion of sex, which you thus pursued with a wild determination that startled your fellow students and shocked your family. Even I, isolated and sheltered as I was by my own introversion, had heard of your behavior, and when I found you watching me, it sent such a rush of fear and embarrassment through my body that I trembled in your presence and was hardly able to speak.

When you told me later of your near drowning, of your humiliation and of your years of nightly plans, it was the persistence of your anger that impressed me—that and the cruelty of your grandfather. It did not occur to me that you might possess a small arsenal, or that this filial betrayal had instilled in you a fundamental mistrust. Nor did it occur to me that your profession might have grown directly from the circumstances of this insult. I am trying to put the pieces together, Jhed. There is so much I do not understand.

It began quite innocently with a search, an archaelogical dig. And then we found the bones. The entire skeleton packed in the dried mud like a fossil. And we knew this was not the only one. There were many. Many babies buried here. After closer examination we determined the skeleton to be that of a five-year-old child. As we continued to wipe the dust and dirt and debris away from the area, we discovered also the tracks of lost animals, prints perfectly preserved in the hard clay pack of the hillock.

On an upper floor, in the therapeutic bath, where everyone was submerged up to their necks in hot water, so that they appeared simply as disembodied heads, floating about on the surface, I noticed for the first time the demonic grins on the faces of the attendants and realized with sudden terror they knew. They were responsible. I and the others must escape. It was in this attempt later that night that I found myself under the big sink in the enormous institutional kitchen, crammed amid the damp and pungent boxes of cleansers, detergents, rank sponges and scrubbers, trying to move without a sound through these toward the half-accessible heavy opaque glass window which I might be able to sqeeze through.

You always widened your eyes when you looked closely at things, unlike me, I squint, as if to look closely were like looking into the sun. Your head was angled slightly down over the pieces spread out before you. You hadn't noticed me, standing in the doorway watching you. I remember it all—the curved neck of the lamp, the dull tan of the formica work table, the precision hand tools. It saddened me to think of everything changing. My vision blurred, and as I brought it back into focus, I saw what you were working on and realized, of course, there was that smell I loved, the smell that reminded me of sewing machine oil. But it wasn't sewing machine oil, it was gun oil. That smell went all the way back to my childhood, to the long blue-black barrel of a .22

rifle, to my father, whose gun it was. I took a step toward you, and you looked up. I couldn't tell if you were glad to see me, there was so much tension between us.

"I've re-blued it," you said. "Come and see." I walked to the table. "Look." You turned the delicate piece of metal in your hands. "See this edge? It was scratched, so I filed it. Then I re-blued it. You can't even tell, can you? Only an expert would know."

"Would you know?" I asked. I was watching your hands, the light gleaming off the fine dark hairs on your fingers.

"Yes," you said. "But I did it." You laughed. You were pleased with yourself, satisfied with your work. Good work, I knew. Your work was very good. Only an expert would know.

The parts of the gun lay on the table. You began putting it back together. You dropped the interior safety deftly into place, then laid the side-plate over the frame and set the first of three small screws. You went on, explaining the process for me. Finally you slid the grip up over the frame and tightened the last screw.

"That's it," you said. You placed the revolver carefully on the formica. I turned. You reached for me and caught my wrist. "Don't go," you said, "you just got here."

"Jhed." I looked down at you, and you held me there.

"You used to sit and talk with me here. Stay now."

"Let me go, Jhed." I felt your fingers loosen their grip. You dropped your hand.

"Lila, what's wrong. Tell me."

It could be mine, this child in my arms. We stare into each other's eyes, rapt as lovers. Now I'm holding a handful of long white feathers, the strong feathers, with thick quills that come only from wings or tail, flight feathers. The feathers of an orphan, with no one to teach it to fly. But it will learn, and it will leave to catch up with those that have flown ahead. I greet this realization with a surprising lack of sadness. I feel only awe and puzzlement.

III

Room after empty room. Cool concrete floors, thick white-washed walls, windows shuttered against the noon heat.

My mother shows me from room to room. This place reminds me of a dairy. These are the kind of rooms that keep milk cool. And these are rooms for work, rooms like a blank page that invites the pen.

Cool, quiet, empty, white rooms—virgin rooms, rooms for creation.

I had come north alone this time and did not know how long I would stay. The tea roses were already in bloom when I arrived. As soon as I got there, I painted the east room of the house. White, like the rooms in my dream. And the early sun splashed the walls with leaf shadows. The room was alive with changing light. Here I worked. In the cool morning I practiced, and the notes of my cello filled the empty room. At last my solitude gave sound to itself—liquid, joyous, lonely, and ultimately elusive as the fluent shadows that graced the white walls.

I waited for the distance to feel comfortable, allowing the gap to widen slowly like the opening of an expanse of water between the dock and a departing ship. I did not think I wanted it too wide to reach across. But I kept drifting and felt only a certain slow relief, like the release of breath in a sigh. Time passed, and still I made no plans.

When I thought of you it was with affection, but without desire. Though I loved your body, the way you touched me, there was a deeper desire I did not feel, a place that could make room for you with longing, which was closed and small as a womb without a fetus to press it open. I was not sure if it was you I missed, or simply the habit of our life together. We had known each other so long, since I was a child, really.

My sadness was without longing, a condition in itself, like being tired, needing sleep, and I had slept long enough. I did not want to escape even this, for if I slept to escape my sadness, I would lose the sun, the small birds in the flowering quince, whose quick bodies contained the essence of some vitality I knew was mine also, which I wanted to reclaim. I would reclaim it. I would not sleep. I would embrace what was real, the truth. If there was a thorn, let it prick me. Let the drop of blood bejewel my finger. I would lick it away, tasting my own salty blood.

I had never seen Angelina's face, but I could imagine it. I had only seen her scurry ahead down the lane one time, darting out of sight through the high fields of wild radish, lavender and white blossoms waving in the wind. She wore a cotton print dress of tiny flowers, faded so that the colors were as pale as the wild flowers around her, and she seemed to belong in the fields with them. She had a scarf over her hair, tied like the women from the old country, and she moved with a certain darting energy, like a small bird. Up the stairs she went, between the wild roses, then down the lane and onto the narrow path that led to the old house almost invisible in the midst of the tall grass and surrounding orchard. Almost invisible, not because it was so small, but because it was old, amid the newer homes that dotted what was once all fields and orchards; and beside the new young places, like the faded dress, it blended into the landscape. But I noticed it, having seen the old woman just that once, climb quickly up the stairs amid the blossoms dancing in a bright spring breeze.

Over and over I saw the figure of this woman, winding her way hastily up the stairs, disappearing down the lane, and this image set upon me an enchantment. Slowly, as I saw the scene again and again, a vision that entered my mind at odd moments during the following days, I began to believe that there was a connection between us, that this woman's presence in my life, so close by, my nearest neighbor, was not coincidence, but destiny. I was not surprised then to find one day not long after, among the assorted pieces of mail in my box, a letter addressed to Mrs. Angelina Luchesi.

I stared at the envelope, understanding simply that I had received a gift. The gift of her name, Angelina. I imagined her hands on the envelope. They would be strong and lightly freckled, like my own, the veins rising out, ridging their backs as mine did sometimes after hours of practice on a particularly difficult piece. Angelina's hands.

The hands of a woman who has worked hard all her life. Still every summer she cans—peaches, apricots, pears, tomatoes, makes applesauce, pickled beets and cucumbers, peppers and eggplant.

Her husband calls her. "Angelina," he says, "what are you doing out there?" He stands at the back door in his undershirt, looking through the square of screen, looking out after her, and she, gone into the garden, barefoot at dawn.

"Angelina!" His voice comes from deep below his chest. He was a bull of a man; he still is. "Angelina!" But she does not answer. She is happy in the garden. The leaves and weeds still wet with dew shake water onto her bare legs as she walks out from the house. She wants to smell the early air, the damp earth. She wants to see the sunflowers.

He watches her. She is still so light on her feet. Still such a wild little thing after all these years, after seven children! He knows she hears him, but she will not answer. All these years and he has not tamed her yet.

It is Saturday. In the afternoon he will woo her. He will put on the old records. Enrico Caruso. Oh how he used to hate that man, he was so jealous! "Angelina," he would shout, "enough Angelina! Take it off! Take the record off the machine. You hear me, Angelina? Take it off!" And she would pretend not to hear, close her eyes and lean back in the chair, smiling. Now he understands. Caruso is dead, no longer a threat. He is an ally, a key to their past, a key to Angelina's heart. The old man turns. He goes into the kitchen. The coffee is ready. His cup is on the table.

It did not for a moment occur to me to write on the envelope, redirecting the letter, and return it to my box for the postman. Nor did it occur to me to walk down to Angelina Luchesi's mailbox and place the letter there. I knew without consideration or doubt that I would take the letter to Angelina's door and deliver it myself.

He seemed to tumble out of the house, to be shaken from it as a penny is shaken from a piggy bank. I was almost to the steps leading up the veranda when the door flew open, slamming back against the outer wall, and he spilled out, all arms and legs and fairly flying, his black hair falling over his face. It was only then, at the same moment he made his inglorious exit, almost at my feet, that I heard voices. "Basta, Luigi, basta!" And he was yelling too, "Mama, Mama, listen to me!" But she would not listen. She must have pushed him right out the door.

I was amazed because he was a big man, bigger than you, Jhed. Not just taller, but heavier, broader shouldered and thicker bodied. He regained his balance and stopped near the bottom of the steps, where he appraised me. He straightened his shirt and collar and very deliberately hitched his pants. I stared at him, too astonished even to feel obligated to speak. He turned his head slowly back toward the door, though Angelina was no longer visible.

"Domani, Mama," he said.

"Mai, mai domani!"

But he wasn't listening. He was already walking past me, fading into the pure sound of the wind. And I had the sensation again of having entered a dream. I turned back to the house, and the old woman was waiting. It seemed she was waiting. I shivered and pulled my sweater together across my light cotton dress. I took the first step up, holding the letter in my hand. Angelina Luchesi looked out at me from the dark of the house. She held open the screen door that had sprung back after Luigi's abrupt departure. "That Luigi," she said, and she held the door open for me.

I was flying. By directing my will I practiced moving upward, out over the water, into the dawn sky. And then I was falling. It was dark and I was falling—a long lightless descent through space, falling, not tumbling, but head-long down. And before I struck the black rocks jutting up from the icy sea below, I gasped and opened my eyes.

The phone was ringing. I reached, frantic to silence it. Out of the awkwardness of sleep, I knocked it off the table. The receiver bounced and skidded across the floor, under the bed. I rolled to the edge of the bed and stretched down. Grabbing the cord and pulling the receiver to me, I captured it as if it were alive. "Hello," I said, breathless and hoarse.

"Lila?"

I was caught off guard, unprepared for the immediacy of your presence. "Oh, Jhed. I'm sorry. I knocked the phone off the table. Did it deafen you?"

"I miss you, Lila."

Guilt sprouted in me like a black seed. I said nothing, but a heaviness spread through my blood so I wanted only to sleep again. The red telephone in my hand was like an alarm, an instrument of emergency—fire or police, pulling me into the present.

Hearing your voice, so familiar and clear, I almost felt you beside me. We had a history of intimate telephone conversations, didn't we Jhed? Before we were married, remember? I used to take the phone into my room so we could talk late at night while I lay in bed, my family asleep down the hall. But now I was alone in an empty house.

"I miss you too." I said it before I could stop myself, and you were only waiting to hear the words before you proposed a meeting.

"I don't know, Jhed." But my caution came too late. I had opened myself, falling into the old closeness. I had not even known I missed you, had not suspected the ache buried beneath the sadness I embraced.

I wanted to say no, but I couldn't. "Yes," I said, amazed that my mouth would move, that my lips would shape the word.

I arrived at the airport early and went to the gate to wait for my plane, choosing a seat in the empty row of orange molded plastic chairs facing the window. In the seat beside me was an abandoned copy of the morning paper. I had seen the headlines earlier as I passed the coffee shop: MIDEAST CRISIS DEEPENS. I had not wanted to read further, but now I felt a sudden desire to know what was happening in the world, as if this would fortify me for our meeting. I picked up the front page, but I was too anxious to actually read the articles. I stared vaguely at the areas of darker print: Woman's Body Found, Social Security Collapse, Beringer Indicted in Nuclear Accident. I let the paper rest for a moment in my lap before I laid it aside and set my mind adrift, gazing out the huge plate glass window onto the series of runways where planes moved about slowly like enormous insects in another world. It reminded me of the ant house my brother had kept with the glass wall. In barely an hour I would be with you again. My mouth was dry. My face felt strange. I tested it, smiling into the expanse of glass and concrete.

The headache came swiftly, like a blow at my temple that turned from a sharp piercing pain almost immediately into a dull throb.

IV

"What did your husband do, Mrs. Hashin? What was his business?"

"Oh," I said, understanding now. But why did it matter? I looked up at the investigating officer. I wished I did not have my glasses on. Everything was too clear, too bright. This was familiar. Had I dreamed it? Was I dreaming? The walls were so white, the voices so mechanical, like robots—were they robots? Amplified, they echoed, part of the white noise of the hospital that was happening all around me—all around me, a white hive with white bees buzzing efficiently on their errand of mercy. Mercy. Have mercy, I wanted to say. Dear God, have mercy.

"What did you say, Mrs. Hashin?"

Had I said something? Startled, I seemed to see him for the first time, this black man with the dark coat and tie, the white collar between his dark face and his dark jacket. Did he belong here, so dark in all this white? Yes, he too was doing his job efficiently, politely. If I gathered myself toward him it would be over sooner. I looked him full in the face. "I'm sorry," I said. "My husband," I hesitated, then continued carefully, forcing myself to say each word precisely and clearly. "My husband was a consultant, a security systems analyst. He had his own business." I stopped, unable to continue in this way, speaking so dispassionately about you, as if you were someone else, not my husband at all, but a stranger.

"Yes, Mrs. Hashin?"

I felt an urgency I did not understand, a question I could not answer. I wanted to satisfy him so that he could make sense of what had happened. "My husband," I groped for words, "my husband," and then it came to me. I shoved the words out in a kind of triumph. "He was an expert," I said, as if somehow this explained everything. I felt myself crumbling then. My shoulders sagged forward. The officer leaned over me, his dark shape sharp against the white walls, the white roar of the fluorescent light, the polished asphalt tile of the emergency room. I was dizzy and suddenly very cold. His face seemed so close, his concern pressing in on me. I took a step back and felt the wall behind me. "Please," I said. "Please."

A haze, of fine gold powder falls gently over everything, and I seem to be floating through it, almost swimming. It's a lazy kind of light, a slow motion feeling, and yet I know I'm moving quickly. I can't feel the ground, only the sensation of weightlessness that carries me, the effortlessness of my momentum. I'm flying.

I'm flying again, like before. I'm flying and the world is golden light and gentle movement, a warm wind is with me, brushing the hair from my forehead.

I'm hit! Slammed into something—solid, dark. Hit face first, then the whole body. I feel nothing. Numbness. No more light, no more warm air, no slow motion swimming, no flying without gravity. Only a crushed limpness as I slide down, down, down against this solid wall. Down, down as I sink and I'm under now, and it's cold, this water that closes over my head as I slide still farther down the slab of dark.

So many years I dreamed those fingers, snakes, worm tongue. I pushed against the squirming things that were always reaching for me, attempting to enter something—my car, my room, my mouth. I was always pushing back, trying to close the door, till at last I dreamed that Angelina took the butcher knife and cut them off, those furtive alien fingers, as I severed the bodies of the worms, digging, preparing the soil for a garden. Is it always so? Must there always be some death to make room for life?

For years I've been pushing back, a token resistance. I've been in retreat. I walked around the house with my glasses off in a kind of fuzz, and I found it restful. I protested softly, easily erased, a woman like soft white chalk on a blackboard. You were solid. I was permeable. You kept the doors locked. So long as I had you I would never have to confront the murder in myself.

But now I have seen these squirming severed bodies in the rich soil steaming with spring. They struggle, to reinsert themselves in the earth's womb. It shocked me to see them. Because it's not true what they say that each end regenerates, not earthworms. When you cut them they die, and the ground here is full of them. I can't tell you how many I've killed.

I remember distinctly, once you said it would be a mess to put a bullet through your temple. A mess, you used that word. And when I asked you why, you told me. Because of what it would do to the body—hydrostatic shock that would jelly the brain. I remember you said the eyes would pop out, just like they do in the mice in the traps I set. I remember because I wanted to know. I remember because it was after I lost the baby. And it was before the International Disarmament Action. I remember because I wanted to know in case. . . . In case, I did tell you that—if there were nothing else to be done, the suffering was pointless. I asked you, and you told me. I had heard of people botching the job. I remember you said it would be awful to find someone like that.

So how could you do that to yourself? No matter what they say, I can't believe it. But I'll never know, will I? Because if you didn't, then who did? And why don't they tell me? Surely they must know.

I can't answer these questions. I've been waiting. I wanted you to tell me. There must be a way you could tell me. Is it because I am not to know? Am I to question myself finally, not you?

Blue. Gun-metal blue. The bluing, you called it. Only an expert would know you had blued, it, or reblued it. The gun—it seemed too big to call a pistol—had been lying on the table before you, the small mechanism, part of the firing mechanism, in your hands. You were showing me the bluing you had done. It was not a pistol, I thought, not a pistol but a gun, big enough to kill. . . . I did not know what.

You focused closely on the small sharp-edged piece of metal in your hands, absorbed in it. It was in your control, this gun. You could take it apart and put it together, load it, fire it, clean it, and put it away. It was under your control.

I was not under your control. You wanted me there with you, but I was not under your control.

Blue. Gun-metal blue. A .44 magnum is a big gun. A .44 can kill a wild pig at 300 yards. It had been under your control, all that power over life and death.

Your attention focused on the small firing mechanism. But your mind wandered, I thought. Your mind was not under your control.

"Don't leave," you said.

But I was not under your control. Only the gun. You could put it together, load it, fire it, clean it and put it away, with careful precise hands, in a way that you could not control even yourself.

Finally it was because of the mice. Because there were so many of them, and there was no one to do it for me.

I set the traps each night, hoping to drift off before I heard the heavy metallic snap announce another small death. But they invaded my sleep. My dreams were violent, and I recalled them vividly. There was one in which you appeared.

I don't know who fired the shot, or even which direction it came from, but suddenly you fell. I saw that the bullet had only grazed your skull, but why then were you so pale, as if your blood had stopped moving or was draining away internally? I had to get you to a hospital right away, and I had to keep you warm. I think that was the last thing you said before you lost consciousness. "Keep me warm." I think you said that.

I put a clear plastic bag over you, with your head out like the hook of a hanger from the dry cleaners, and then I wrapped you in my sleeping bag. The dull army green color and the plastic bag made me think later of war casualties.

At the hospital, running out of time, I begged someone to look at you right away. At last a nurse complied. You were grey and growing colder.

"This man is dying," she pronounced.

"Give him a transfusion," I said.

The bullet had grazed your skull and spiralled down, to lodge itself finally in the femoral artery of your right thigh. Was the bullet removed? Did you live or die?

I woke without knowing.

The night before, *it was a plane spiralling down the dark body of night into the heart of a great city where we were separated by the crowd and washed in panic from doorways to streets to balconies to intersections under neon, knowing any moment the plane would shoot out of the darkness and explode amid the inescapable concrete.*

I met a man who reminded me of my brother, and under the threat of immi-

nent death felt a passionate tenderness, a sweet desire as I leaned against him in the
dark, the rough wool of his shirt scratching my cheek.
    "So, you're back," you said, when you found me, and I was instantly
angry.

The plane never crashed. The scene changed. But in the morn-
ing there was another dead mouse.

Every morning another dead mouse. I set the traps with peanut
butter, because it's sticky and has to be licked off the delicate tooth of
the trigger that releases the spring so the solid metal bar flies forward. I
smeared the peanut butter over the tiny prong with the end of a match-
stick before I set the pin and placed the trap on the floor beside the
stove.

Sometimes it did not strike their backs, breaking their spinal
cords so that they felt nothing. No, sometimes it caught them across
the head and their eyes popped out, or it crushed their skulls and their
little mouths were squashed sideways, the needle teeth starkly white
against the pale pink gums.

Their whiskers were long and black, their fur was grey-gold and
silky, their bellies were pale, and the feet reminded me of the hands of
newborn babies with their perfect sharp paper-thin fingernails.

In the morning I gathered my courage and looked. Another dead
mouse. It took me several steps to dispose of them. At first I did noth-
ing, only looked and went away. Later I picked up the trap, the mouse
now stiff, and placed it on the back steps. Still later, after I had fortified
myself with tea, perhaps even listened to the morning news, I got
around to taking out the garbage. At this point I confronted the trap—
the dead mouse with its lovely little body, its miraculous ears. I did not
allow my aesthetic appreciation to complete itself. This was a dead
mouse. This was nothing to do with me. I pried the tight bar upward
against the spring, and the mouse slid out, falling to the step with a soft
dull thud.

There seemed to be so many of them. Was this seven, or eight? I
had never expected so many. One mouse, I had thought, maybe two.
That night I heard the trap spring early and had to alter my pro-
cedure. The trap had to be set again, because the others would come

out. The others. How many were there? I wanted it to end. I felt like a sniper picking off innocent villagers one by one as hunger drove them from hiding.

I found my slippers in the dark, and then the flashlight. The mouse was a small one. One eye had already greyed in the center. But I had the uneasy feeling it might not be dead. I did not want to touch it, knowing it would still be warm. I crouched in the doorway and opened the trap. The mouse fell silently through the light rain onto the step. I straightened and closed the door, shook my head, as if to shake off death itself, and went about the grim business of resetting the trap.

The next morning, I found another mouse in the trap. The first mouse was still on the steps, its fur soaked and clinging to the fragile body, half its head gnawed away, by what I wondered, stunned at the clean pink of the torn flesh. I was about to pry the bar up from across the body of the second mouse when it wagged its tail. I dropped the trap. The mouse's tail wagged again, and a foot twitched. I had a moment of clear horror before it came to me, a story my father once told. I got the bucket, filled it with water, and plopped the mouse and trap in, thinking that would be a merciful end. But no, the wooden trap floated and the mouse bobbed up and down on the surface. I had to find a weight—the hammer—and put the head of the hammer on the trap to weigh it down to the bottom of the bucket. A few bubbles escaped before I left it, too sick to watch the end. It is so deliberate, this killing. I cannot escape responsibility, and I can't help thinking of you. I keep wanting to wake up, as if I were dreaming someone else's nightmare.

I don't bury them. I remind myself that they are food for something, as I will someday be, and this thought comforts me. So unlike you, my dear, with your clean ashes. How I wish I could have planted you like a small seed. And then I would have placed over your body the tendril roots of what would someday be a great tree. And we could have grown old together after all.

I don't bury the mice. There are too many of them. If we all had to bury our victims, see them die, then would the killing stop? I set the trap again.

V

Angelina brought fresh comfry from the garden and placed the damp leaves on my face, across my swollen cheek, my lacerated ear. She made comfry tea, too, which I drank, tasting little, but grateful for the soothing warmth. All this was later, at the end of what seemed a long journey that began before I can remember.

But some part of me had not walked away from the tangled metal. And I was not certain who it was that walked away, who it was that collapsed, separate from the wreckage, caving into the highway, dazed, but alive.

After a few days they moved me to my own house and I lay watching shadows play on the silent white wall of the room which had so many mornings been filled with the slow sweet notes of my cello.

And you came to me. There was something I had to tell you. Your presence beside me was like a mirage, but more substantial. The light around you wavered like the heat above a strip of highway on a scorching day, or pictures I've seen of salt caravans blurred by the heat of desert sand.

I dreamed it afterward, over and over—the moment just prior to impact, the sensation of *body flopping like a rag, face flattening against the windshield.* Who was I? I was the one who dreamed.

Later I dreamed of *going to the house of the watchmaker, staring into the glass cases, my face unrecognizable—of climbing to the upper floors to see the fabulous collections of silver tea sets, ornate gold goblets, and going down the hall from one luxurious room of treasures to another, seeing a copy of TIME magazine with a black and white photograph on the cover, four or five people, layers of grey, rag-bound, like the soldiers of Napoleon's army retreating from Russia, or the soldiers of any war, the wounded, resting, perhaps dying. The words above the photo identifying the article read: "Getting Free of Life,"* as if this were a new consciousness movement. Who was I? I was the dreamer awakened. I was the survivor, the wounded amid riches, amid perfection, amid art and refinement. I wandered the red carpeted floors from room to room, overwhelmed. Who was I? I was the flawed amid the flawless, I was the snake with new skin, the baby with head bruised by forceps. I did not know who I was.

I did not know who I was, only what I had been, what I had walked away from, what had been left behind in the wreckage of the car.

My self—whole, uninjured, I walked away from that. Myself immortal, I walked away from that. Myself innocent and irresponsible, I walked away from that. I walked away and who was I? I was the woman whose husband had lost his soul. I was the widow who set the trap called Killer. I was a beginning that already knew the end.

There was no one incident, no single day or event. Things change slowly, unnoticed until one day something happens and we realize they're gone. The ending was not the day I left, not the day you died, not the day I crawled out of my car with my face bleeding. There was no real ending, only a constant migration of self in variations on a theme, evolving rhythms.

I couldn't say when the girl I clung to began to grow into a woman. Perhaps it was the moment Angelina laid her rough hand on my forehead and said, "Sleep, sleep. Dorme bene." Perhaps it was when I took the first mouse from the trap, or the moment when you came into my room that morning it seems so long ago. Somewhere something was lost and I did not know what. Something slowly seeped away from me and I could not go back. Finally, I had to let it go.

These seeds—I turn them slowly on my palm, pale and flat and oval as tears. The seeds from Angelina, squash seeds. Zucchini and acorn and patty pan and yellow crook-neck and spaghetti squash.

"They will grow. Si, si," Angelina assured me. "For a woman, the squash will always grow."

I hold the seeds gratefully. They promise so much more than sticky vines and yellow trumpets, more than the fruit they will bear. I slide them into the blue bowl on the table before me and lean back in my chair. I will plant them in the field behind the house, along the stretch of dirt shielded by the bramble of wild roses.

JOURNAL OF A GHOST WATCHER

JOURNAL OF A GHOST WATCHER

I

I WOKE TO SOFT SPLASHING SOUNDS, something next door in the lily pond, a long time, gently, as I lay in bed near the open window, staring into the dark, the cat beside me, ears alert, both of us listening, imagining, each too lazy to get up and look out. My clean-washed hair spread silky on the flowered pillow as I turned my head to breathe the spring night air, grateful to sleep again with the window open, now that winter has passed.

What would I change? Nothing. The cat is here, and whatever it is that plays in the pond, and my neighbors, tucked into their beds at an hour too late even for night owls and late night readers. Earlier I stood on the porch, aware of other open windows, lights on inside, the music of my stereo drifting through the screen door behind me.

Winter kept us closed apart, disconnected. Now that spring has come, we've put away our gloves and our flannel nightshirts. My bare legs in the bed love the smooth sheets and the feel of their skin against each other. The air is once again shared breath.

Buddy and I keep company. He climbs the porch railing to stand beside me, rubs his back against the upright 4 × 4 post, trails the tip of his tail along the lower edge of the awning. Together we watch dusk fall over the alley each evening, watch the windows light up, and breathe the first trace of early jasmine from the next door trellis. To-gether we go in to bed, I under the fluffy blue quilt, he atop it, curled by my side. All night we share the shift of season, the newly opened window. I am the only one of us who speaks.

"What is it, Buddy?" I ask after we've listened awhile to the pond visitor. "A night heron?" In the dark I cannot see his eyes, but his head is lifted, nose pointed toward the window.

Still, we do not go to the window to look. We prefer to imagine. I do not tell Buddy, I have the feeling it could be a young woman out there. She might be naked, playing in the shallow pond. It's almost warm enough for such an adventure. It might be the girlfriend of the red-haired young man who lives one house over, in the back, on the second story. The little pond is just below his window. If it is she, then he is there, too, sitting on the grass in the shadows, watching her. She might only have taken her shoes off and lifted the hem of her dress to wade, barefooted, barelegged. I can almost hear her laughing softly with pleasure at the feel of the cool dark water, the slightly squishy silted bottom between her toes. I do not think till morning, when Jeff calls.

"Raccoon," he says.

"I hadn't thought of that. Of course. More than likely. You're probably right. Raccoon."

By this time, the black tom has already strutted through the alley in his moth-eaten coat on his morning rounds, yowling pitifully for company. He's a friendly fellow and never seems to quarrel with Buddy. Sometimes we find him lounging on our stairs. I think he's lonely. I think he's puzzled by this end of the block, which is jam-packed with cats, all of whom have been neutered, save himself and one other tom named Taffy because of his long pale orange coat.

There was briefly yet a third tom, part Siamese, who for several days running wandered around the yard spraying more frequently than I had thought possible. One morning he did this four times in less than five minutes, the final event occurring inches away from Buddy's nose as he lay benignly on the step just above the walkway. I last saw Mr. Siam in the bushes along the lane. When I coaxed him out, he let me pick him up, purring and rather limp in my hands. I noticed then that his formerly impressive fuzzy chocolate balls had been shaved and stitched. Haven't seen him since. I felt a bit sad for him, he had been so brazen!

The lilac is blooming. It was just this time a year ago I learned its history—how Leonard had planted it for his wife. It was his daughter who told me this while Leonard lay on his death-bed in the hospital. Everything has changed now, and I am the only one here who knows the story of that lilac. It occurred to me that perhaps the woman at the pond last night was she, Leonard's dead wife. How strange it must seem to her, coming back to all of us. She must wonder where her children have gone—and what has happened to the house where I live now, on the top floor, up the stairway which ends at my narrow covered porch.

Leonard's wife remembers how it was, remembers the day Leonard planted that lilac for her. It was only a foot or two tall then. Now it's higher than the tops of the downstairs windows, the fragrant blossoms a froth of lavender swaying in the breeze. It must have been planted nearly thirty-seven years ago, because Mary was thirteen when her mother died. Now she's married and had her first baby, and she and her husband have moved away. He got training as an appliance repairman. "There's steady money it it," he said. "You can work for a company with benefits." I've picked some of that lilac. It's in a hand-blown vase from Portugal on the table in the living room.

Was it the lilac that made me dream of my first husband? We walked together as the dead must walk in heaven, reunited, companionably strolling arm in arm, in perfect step, in perfect understanding. Just so, Leonard and his wife might walk now. But perhaps not, for if she comes to the pond at night, she comes alone, I'm certain. And she comes just when the lilac is blooming, though I suppose she could have come before, and I never noticed. Only now, with my newly opened window, I can hear her out there.

Taffy has been here a long time. I'm sure Mary once told me he was her mother's cat. That makes him nearly as old as I am, very old for a cat. He has blue eyes, and an odd way of watching us, suspiciously, as if he knew we did not belong here, as if he resented the way things have turned out. He must miss her caresses. He's grown wild and cantankerous, the terror of the neighborhood feline population. If she were alive, he would be gentle, he would be better fed and fatter, he would not run when I come down the stairs.

The lilac is on the south side of the house, bordering the neighbors slightly downhill, or perhaps they only seem downhill because their house is a single story, and so my living room window looks out over their roof. "They" are a couple and their small black dog. The dog is always running off and she has to call and call. Even so, it doesn't come back unless it wants to. She has a rose garden. The roses aren't blooming yet, but it won't be long. I see the two of them puttering in the yard. It looks inviting when she comes out in summer in the morning, wearing shorts and rubber thongs to water. She drags the hose along, leaving dark wet patches on the concrete walk that glisten when the light hits them. I hear their voices. The dog howls when they leave it home alone. And it howls when the fire sirens go off. The fire station is only three blocks from here, and all summer, especially toward the end, the day is punctuated by fire alarms.

Coming into the living room at night, as always I glance at the window, the long pane of uncurtained glass through which I see the lights of town. What do I expect? Could there be anyone there? Someone on stilts? Jack half-way up the beanstalk? What I see, not surprisingly, is myself, a ghostly image reflected and transparent, a revenant. I cross to the far side of the window to let the shade down, edging past the split leaf philadendron, whose leaves nearly touch the descending slat-bamboo blind. "Pardon me," I say, addressing the plant. I don't always lower this shade and therefore do not always notice the plant so directly. When I do, I always greet it. Sometimes I say, "Hello."

The room is pleasant and cozier with the bamboo over the black glass. Now the room is self-contained. It could be somewhere else, not a suburban town, maybe New York. I often think, when I look out over the lights at night, of New York, a vague drifting sort of thought. And I'm aware that it has something to do with my sister, whose presence is behind me from the large painting on the north wall, a portrait she painted, in which we merge, she and I, to make a presence larger than life, impossible to ignore, like my sister herself. This undoubtedly contributes to the rather grand, albeit fleeting, sense of my living room as a penthouse.

The kettle steams in the kitchen, having reached a rolling boil. If it were the hot chocolate I had forgotten it would have boiled over and begun by now to ooze down through the stove's innards. Lucky it was only the kettle. I like a steamy kitchen. What was that story my friend told about a woman who, just before her husband arrived home, would put a pot of water on to boil, which created the illusion of dinner in preparation?

Buddy lolls in my path on the carpet, looks up at me, and rolls, exposing his sleek black belly. He eyes me as I step across him, stretches langorously, and reaches one paw to catch the heel of my slipper. This is an attempt at seduction, but I must turn the kettle off before the water boils away. I pass a pile of books on the table by the counter, reach for one, and carry it with me to the kitchen to read while the tea brews.

The moon is nearly full now and fills my room with light the night long, softly spreading through the white blinds, not warm like the sun with its lemony glow, but a magical silver. And since it is night, the time when objects especially take on their own life, a mysterious expectancy inhabits the room when I turn out my bedside lamp or wake from dreams. Surely Leonard's wife slips in among the shadows in the garden on such nights. Surely she too enjoys the moonlight. Yet I have not heard her at the pond again. I suppose the moon is too bright there, and she is wary of being seen among the luminous camellia blossoms and starry marguerites. Still, she must come to smell the lilacs. Their perfume rises in the air through my open windows in the warm darkness.

The woman who moved into Jim's old apartment keeps her curtains drawn at night, sensibly, since unlike myself, she lives on the ground floor; and people troop past her door at odd hours, unpredictably. Buddy and I listen from our relative invisibility, waiting for a clue, a familiar voice or revealing conversational reference, the turn of a lock, or sound of a door opening—events which would signal the presence of a neighbor. But sometimes it seems the voices or footsteps belong to transients, strangers passing through along the walkways, either the one on my side of the fence, which I consider, in fact, my walkway, or the one that parallels the other side of the fence and then meanders an east-west axis through the lawns and shrubs, between the rear apartments, and along the side of the house next door, right past Jim's old front door.

The woman who has moved there must feel vulnerable with her windows and door opening onto that walkway. During the day, she draws the curtains aside, and I have seen, on the table by the window, a vase of pink camellias she must have picked from the garden. Today I noticed the petals of one blossom had fallen and lay spilled around the vase, bright against the dark surface of the round table.

My own house has flowers in every room. I read somewhere that nothing brings a room to life like fresh flowers, and my rooms are proof of this. Take the flowers out and one feels an absence, a sense of loss, as if someone had gone away.

What does Leonard's wife feel when she comes home and finds none of her family left? Perhaps she looks in my windows and sees the flowers, so that the house once filled with seven children seems less empty than it would otherwise. She is rooted here, and here she chooses to stay, in spirit at least, rather than moving on into that other infinitude. Of reunions I cannot guess. Perhaps she is not ready yet to be reunited with her husband. Perhaps, like myself, she chooses to linger in the recovered freedom of her separate state, as if unmarried, a girl again, virgin and young, feeling the grass between her toes, sliding her feet slowly into the cool pond.

We are supposed to rush away from this state, to plunge toward matrimony as one would toward salvation or heaven. But she tarries here, as I do, savoring the sweet spring, puzzled perhaps by the absence of her children, but perhaps not. Perhaps she does not look for them at all, only enjoys the peace and quiet of her privacy and the pleasure of recollection in her own time, on her own terms.

There is little enough time for that, for the re-creation of the past we do when we have time to remember at leisure. Surely this is one of life's pleasures, akin to reverie, the dreaming into dying fires our ancestors have done since time immemorial. I think of my mother, of the continuum of life she passed to me. As athletes pass the torch? A rather dramatic perspective, to think of oneself rushing forward with the flame, preparing to pass it to another generation.

But I have no daughter. The flame stops here. And though I miss having that daughter I would have cherished and adored and loved and hated as only a mother can, perhaps it is best. I have no one to achieve for, no path to light for kin to follow. I am free to be here with less ambition; life is more of a limbo present. I look back rather than forward, when it comes to blood relations. Is this how it is for Leonard's wife, now that she is dead and the race is over? Is that why I feel I understand her? She's crossed the finish line and now returns to explore the terrain she hardly had time to notice.

Leonard's wife could have waited for her husband without confusion, though I suspect she has waited for no one. I have no such clarity, for if our spouses reunite with us in the life hereafter, then one who widowed me waits there already, while several more (who might not wish at all to spend life ever-lasting with me) will, at some point, arrive. At least one may spare me further concern and join his present wife when the occasion arises, if such a plan follows the laws of succession, in which case the last will be the ones we abide with in eternity. But I have some question about that, since it seems as likely the rule might be first instead of last, and no answers at all.

I think of my mother's mother more and more often as I feel myself drawing closer to her. She died when I was nine, and for years my thoughts of her were brief memories, vivid and discontinuous. Over time I have knitted a pattern for her and she has become more whole, inextricably part of my life, of who I am. Without my being quite aware of it, as I grew older, I began to see her in a larger context—beloved daughter, wife, mother, and solitary woman amid a large and boisterous family which included more grandchildren than I can at the moment count. There were lots of cousins.

I understand now what she must have known then—how we move toward the dead. There must be a point at which we straddle both worlds, the reality of each in perfect balance. That is the point at which I would like to stay, poised there, in contact with the living, with the joy and wonder of spring, of passion, of life entering this world, all the while aware of the point where the balance tips and we slide into the world that awaits beyond this. Leonard's wife has chosen to keep them both, for here she is among the remnants of her history, on this earth, in this house, this garden.

I do not sense in her a longing, rather a pleasure taken in the sensate world, which she chooses not to forfeit but to taste again, as one might bite into a lush plum with all the anticipation of pleasure derived from the plums of memory, of fantasy—this plum, not only itself, but the many, the ideal.

My grandmother, to my knowledge, does not return. But how am I to know? Her house was sold. No family lived on there after her, but scattered to the four winds like so much thistle down, across oceans, mountains, deserts, connected now by telephone, more ghostly in each other's lives than Leonard's wife is to me here, no closer to me now than my grandmother herself, from wherever she has gone beyond my apprehension.

The sun this morning blazed the white wall of the apartment behind mine where the young couple live. The shadows were so sharp you could have followed their outline with a pencil. Dew drops no bigger than the head of a pin with their infinitesimal weight drooped the tips of bamboo leaves in the planter on my porch. There is such precision in the temporal, the transient.

Buddy followed me out and lay on the top step near me as I listened to the dawn birds flutter in the oleander. My grandmother's house was surrounded by oleander. That was where I first heard the word. Oleander. It meant only that then, those bushes with the pink and white blossoms and milky sap that edged her lawn. Oleander. Now it is like the plum Leonard's wife tastes. My grandmother's oleander superimpose themselves on these oleander. I carry my past with me, and no one sees it, just as the lilac is only that lilac to everyone but me, since the others do not know how it came to be here.

Yesterday I saw the young man who lives upstairs in back. It was the first time I've seen him outside. He walked up the path past Jim's old apartment. Though I've still never seen his face, this time I saw his thick red hair, his broad back, and the bag of dry cleaning slung over one shoulder. Moments after he disappeared, Taffy emerged from the bushes just beyond the edge of the lawn. He stuck his tail straight up and backed into the low green leaves with that wild look he gets and spent a long minute leaving his mark. Buddy and I observed this from the porch. Buddy sat gravely alert, his fur dusty in the afternoon sun; and when I turned to go back into the house, he rose and turned with me. "Buddy," I said, "you really can't keep rolling in the dirt like that and expect to come in." He brushed past me into the kitchen, clearly unconcerned with my ideas of cleanliness. "What about that Taffy cat?" I asked. But he didn't answer.

Now the alley is overgrown with nascent leaves whose texture is still tender and pliable. The morning air is cool and the breezes stir the lithe young branches. They bend and sway, arching invitingly over the alley. I think of little girls, their long hair, ribbons and sashes streaming behind them as they run through the bushes and over the narrow paths. I see myself as I was, with my cousins, my brothers and sisters, and Leonard's children, too. We are a tribe of children, equalled in this neighborhood only by the multitude of cats. There is a joy in this imagining, joy and a slight sense of loss, for indeed, here there are no children running rampant through the alley, their laughter on the wind, only the promise of a place for them which remains unfilled.

Last week there was a baby downstairs. At first I thought I hadn't noticed Jean was pregnant. She's a large woman with rounded shoulders. I could imagine her being pregnant and my not noticing—but nine months pregnant?

It turned out a homeless couple was staying temporarily with her and Terry. That explained the VW camper parked in the driveway. The camper bothered me, actually. Though I felt sympathetic to the couple and their baby, I found it disconcerting to have them virtually living in our parking place. It seemed sordid. He was very thin with long stringy hair. He wore faded yoga pants and t-shirts, all of which looked rumpled and spotted. She was quite pretty, also with long straight hair only slightly better kept than his. The baby cried a lot. I imagine they ate brown rice, most certainly not meat, probably Tahini butter on their dry multi-grain bread. I would pull into my parking spot beside their van with its open side door and try not to intrude by looking in.

After a week or so they moved on, hopefully to something better than another parking space, though Terry and Jean had them in the house, where they were able to shower and cook and do their laundry. Jean's line was a series of small white diaper sails. I liked hearing the baby at night. "This," I told Buddy, "is not Sebastopol. This is Hong Kong. This is the close quarters of the Orient." The smell of fried tofu drifted up from Jean's kitchen though my attic door. Hong Kong. Tokyo. Maybe Djakarta. And then they were gone.

Several days later I woke in the middle of the night to the smell of coffee from the attic. Jean's really getting up early these days, I thought. Poor woman, her work is endless. And I went back to sleep. The next day Terry asked me if I smelled smoke that night. "Smoke?" I said. "No, I smelled coffee." "No," he said, "Jean forgot she was cooking beans. The whole house filled up with smoke before we woke up. If it hadn't been such a good pot, we might have burned the place down."

I have a long rope with a loop already set in one end and a pair of gloves next to it. I keep these in a basket near my bed, because there's no way out, except my kitchen door. That rope is my fire escape. Seeing it there reminds me of my first husband, the one waiting in heaven, who perished fighting a wildfire in the mountains. I look at that rope in the basket with the pair of garden gloves tucked into its tough fibrous coil, and I remember my plan. I'll make a noose around the framing between windows in my bedroom and lower myself down it, wearing my gloves, of course, to avoid rope burns on my hands. I think how Frank would approve, how he would nod solemnly, much as my own father might, and praise me for my foresight. I imagine him watching from that other world, glad to see that I will do my best not to go up in smoke myself.

Before Jean and Terry and the kids moved in, I used to hear Leonard down there late at night sometimes drunk and hollering. When his sons came to dinner, I went out. I spent the night at friends, because when the Kearny boys got together, the fireworks started about eleven and went on till dawn. Sometimes Mary called the police. Even when Leonard wasn't drinking, I could hear him cough. He had a deep voice, passed on to all his sons. One night when the fighting started I heard Mary's voice. She must have said something about me, because her brother, the one who was the worst when he drank, that brother, whose name I can't remember, said, "The hell with her. I don't care if she hears me." He bellowed this.

Sometimes I hear Terry and Jean. And of course I hear the children when they get wild. Terry has a quiet voice, and his words are inaudible, a murmur, though occasionally he crashes around, and it sounds like they're moving furniture at midnight, which they probably were at first. Jean told me Terry is a night owl and often wants to discuss the world's problems in the wee hours when she would rather sleep. She herself has a shrill voice and is going through a stage with her oldest daughter, a willowy and sullen teenager. Once a week or so they have a great fight with much yelling and slamming of doors. I find this as painful as I found Leonard's arguments with his sons and their arguments with each other, though fortunately Jean and her daughter seem to confine their conflicts to mid-morning, usually on Saturdays.

Oh, after Leonard died there were some doozies! The funeral was followed by a big wake. This went on for twenty-four hours. Gradually friends of the family faded and departed, leaving the children and their families. Then the brothers went at it. This lasted another two days, then intermittently for several weeks as they argued over how to divide the estate—whether to sell the house. All this Leonard's wife witnessed, of course. I wonder if it distressed her? It distressed Taffy. Something did during that time, because he yowled all night and scratched at the windows.

Buddy was fit to be tied. They'd have these stand-offs, Buddy on the inside, every hair on end, Taffy on the outside, equally puffed, his blue eyes narrowed to nasty slits, his teeth gleaming, the two of them not more than three inches apart, with only the clear pane of glass dividing them. Between the cats and the Kearnys, you wouldn't have believed the racket. Jim was still here then, and he told me it had been going on for years. Even over at his place he used to hear the fights.

Thank God, Jean and Terry don't have a television. I used to hear the Kearny's TV constantly. On a quiet night, when I couldn't hear much but Leonard's groaning and coughing, I'd hear the TV from his room at the back of the house, the room Terry and Jean's daughter has now. I can't help wondering what the neighbors hear of me. They must hear when I have company. Other random sounds which might be startling: when I drop things in the bathroom, which I do only very early in the morning or very late at night, half asleep or dead tired—the jar of face cleanser, which makes a resounding whack when it strikes the linoleum tile; the lids to various creams and lotions; my hair brush; the telephone, which I'm always dragging around the house, continuing a conversation while I wash the dishes or load the laundry.

Last night the neighbor's dog, Max, zoomed across the alley on Buddy's heels. All the while his mistress called, "Max, Max! Come home, Max," as she always does when he leaves the yard. It surprised me that he actually did turn and go home, just at the bottom of my stairs, which Buddy had by-passed like a torpedo, a mere two feet ahead of him. It was a particularly strange sight, since Max is as black as Buddy, but five times larger, and they flew across the yard nearly atop each other.

Imagine a huge black creature hurtling through the last twilight, discernible in the dusk merely as a shape, a coalescence of darkness, heard before seen, clawed paws tearing across the gravel, and when seen, only then, another smaller concentration of darkness visible slightly ahead of it, the latter being Buddy, who continued his flat-out escape, careening around the corner of the house and disappearing just as Max screeched to a stop, turned, and trotted in the opposite direction back home.

Walking in the alley today I noticed for the first time their secret passages, the places they nest as one might not imagine a cat would, rounded hollows in the vine and hedge between the alley and the neighbors to the west, also a smaller tunnel further down, leading in and presumably out the other side, though not straight through of course, for cats ever prefer a meandering route even when they know exactly where they're going. This was a comforting discovery, these passages where no doubt a host of intrigue has its place—trysts and quarrels, hostile stand-offs and intimate gossip. I understand now how it is that often when I drive in and find a cat or two lolling about on the warm pavement, they can seem to strangely evaporate, slipping, I now know, into these leafy grottos, out of sight in a wink, safe from harm, just as the wheels of my car reach the spot where a moment before one of them was lying. A cat's reaction time is one three-hundredth of a second!

There were no cats out today when I walked through, the unseasonable north wind breathing down my neck, in spite of my jacket collar turned up. Clouds scudded in great billows from the northwest, and I thought surely it would storm, though the sun broke through in clear patches of bright blue sky. My, but it was cold! The cats, I presumed, had taken refuge where they could, knowing what was coming, and sure enough, at six-thirty this evening, the sky broke with a freezing rain, and I felt that cold against my back again, though I had the house around me and a cup of hot tea to sip.

Like the cats, Leonard's wife must take shelter where one would never think to find her. Under the house? But no, she's far too free a spirit to confine herself to any dark shut-in place. She's much more likely to find shelter in an arbor, or a thick-leafed overhanging branch—perhaps someone's porch, where she might whisper to the occupant who came out a moment to watch the weather. Yes. She might blow on a person's ear or down their neck like that northwind; and when they turned quickly, the hair at the back of their heads prickling, she would, of course, be invisible.

I imagine her laughing, a generous warm laugh of pure amusement at her invulnerability, her power to tease with complete impunity, knowing she cannot be seen, unless she chooses, except by some. Yes, by some, for I can see her. I would recognize her there, under the arbor, or in the half-light of the porch. She is so young and wild, now that she is alone. She tosses her long hair and her eyes dance with a nearly wicked merriness. Then again, she might just as soon leave the arbor, the leaves, the porch and dance out into the rain, for she never minds the cold. Her thick hair would rope the water down. Her clothes would soon be soaked and stick to her body. Wouldn't she turn her face up into the rain? Wouldn't she challenge the gods themselves?

When I rose at five-thirty this morning, the only light on was from the woman who lives directly below the red-haired young man. I have heard that she complained when the young man found a girlfriend. It seems they carried on at night, made all sorts of noise, she said, at all hours! She was shocked, disgusted, imposed upon. How could he! She spoke to him about it. Ann, their next-door neighbor, was called upon to arbitrate. How this was resolved, I do not know;

but from my porch at night, I have seen the young man and his girl-friend, never all of them at once, but his shoulders, her hands, the side of his head, her blond hair; and I have gone back into my house, happy for them, curious, retreating only because their intimacy calls for a decent respect, as ours does, you know. We turn off the porch light, Jeff and I; but anyone watching would see us there, in the dark-ness, perhaps outlined by the light from inside.

We must pretend we are in Japan and look away from the neigh-bors as if we did not see. I'm told on a Tokyo subway you could scream and, out of politeness, none of the other passengers would look up from their newspapers. It would seem you had not uttered a sound. Tokyo. Djakarta. Hong Kong. Manila. The cries of a baby heard through thin walls, the rising voices of drunken men, the smell of coffee at 3:00 a.m. We could have burned the house down, Terry said. Buddy sniffs the chair, yowls at Taffy. To the south my neighbor calls her dog. "Good boy, good boy," she praises when he comes. The fire department siren goes off. The lilac blossoms fade to a withered white. Leonard's wife slips into the shadows. The children vanish in the alley, and green branches fold their secrets into themselves.

II

Last night I couldn't sleep, and for the first time in many nights, I heard her again at the pond. She must have been there very briefly, because I heard just one clear splash, quiet as the others have been, as if she had merely slid one foot into the water. "Jeff, did you hear that?" But you were sleeping. I lay very still, hoping to hear more. But the yard was silent, and I did not go to the window, certain she would resent my intrusion. I don't think anyone else knows that she comes, and if they did, she might grow even wilder, like Taffy, wily and more elusive than ever. After all, this is still her home, she ought to feel at liberty to come and go. Taffy came to the bottom of the steps earlier last night. "Look at his eyes," I said, "see how strange they are," — blue and close together and almost crossed. And he stared up as if we were completely alien, as if he had never seen a human being before.

You walked to the edge of the porch to see, but Taffy took off around the corner and was gone.

The weather has grown dry and hotter by the day and the wild bulbs with their fireworks of white blossoms faded much sooner than last year. Their long green foliage fell limp and yellowing in the flower bed and over onto the walkway, so I pulled them up and though the bed looks tidier, it is full of empty spaces where the inhospitable gravel and clay glare up at me.

I stare off at the green pastures outside town, the white tips of fences along the hill, the line of dark trees at the horizon, up into the vague overcast sky. Those waterskates I watched in the creek yesterday were a gift—grace came with them, and I could imagine dying without resistance into that moment of wholeness.

"God forgive me!" I cried out in my dream. I woke up. Forgive me for what, I wonder? What sin had I committed? You slept on, my shore, my solid ground. My common sense, my wariness, my practical and honest dear one, my friend. You slept on, grinding your teeth in your dreams. What were you dreaming, my dearest? My truck, my rock, my ring, my blanket, my harbor—what were you dreaming, grinding your teeth like that, like a glacier grinding down, down? What were you dreaming, riding that ice, those rocks all night while I lay beside you, lost in the recollection of night blooming jasmine, of gardens, of ghosts?

"You missed her," I said in the morning.

"Who?" you asked.

"Leonard's wife. She came to the pond again last night."

It was dark when I woke, but there are birds (I do not know what kind) that converse at that hour. It's not the first time I've heard them. In the night, their warbling and muted whistlings fall through the dark as clear and discrete as falling drops of water. Sometimes their voices crowd each other, over-lapping and tumbling in a-rhythmic harmonies and the outright dissonances of apparent argument. Sometimes they converse more politely, with small silences between their phrases, as if they were giving thought to the subject.

Lying in bed, or from my narrow porch, I listen, certain there is no one else awake, wondering exactly what those birds are talking about and what kind of birds they are anyway. At that hour, the neighborhood is otherwise utterly quiet, the latest traffic of the night having found its way home, the earliest of the morning not yet on the streets. Not a window is lit, and I feel as if I were the only person awake in the whole wide world, never mind that the sun has half the planet up. Sometimes there is comfort in this, sometimes loneliness, and always there is the sense of contact with another world, one I am reluctant to relinquish, that vanishes each day once the sun rises.

In those pre-dawn hours, when the birds speak to one another, I feel absolutely alone and simultaneously connected to all humankind, the living, the dead and the unborn. In those hours I apprehend my place in context, in the generational field, the evolutionary environment that transcends not only family but species. My pulse synchronizes with the pulse of life itself. My breath links with the breathing of the very earth, and I feel I belong where I am.

This minor miracle is all too soon interrupted as another day begins, and I become estranged, fragmented, losing all sense of the entrainment science tells us must always be operative between proximate systems. No wonder Leonard's wife has no interest in lingering here by daylight, with the constant movement of cars and trucks and people bustling about, the ringing of telephones, the humming of electronic devices. She retreats and waits it out.

I stood this morning on the north side of the house, holding the sprinkler over tiny blue and purple faces of forget-me-nots, wild violets, and violas that sprung up through the layers of green leaves along the fence, and thought of her, realizing once again that I do not know her name. And now Mary is gone so there is no one to ask. Then something occurred to me. I suppose because I finally realized (unless Mary and Sean show up unexpectedly as they did that one time) I shall never again have the opportunity to ask. It came to me that Leonard's wife doesn't care. She has become nameless, only herself, a wild spirit, with no interest whatever in a name, in just the way that Taffy has no interest in the name Taffy, does not respond to it in the slightest, thinks of himself if at all, I imagine, as CAT, which in fact suits him far better than Taffy, for he is not in the least domesticated. Nor is she, Leonard's wife. She is long past domestication. She has left domestication behind.

Lately she's been talking to me in a certain way, not directly mind you, not in so many words. But when I imagine her, or see her face shining from the shadows, I understand the universe exists in and of itself, nameless, save for us, or named in another way, the way Indians name things, like the poet whose narrator would name herself "She Who Looks Back." Leonard's wife might have a name like that: "She Who Comes Back To See," or "She Who Joined The Nameless Ones."

I felt, standing there by the fence with the water broken and spilling in a million pieces, that I too might join the nameless, that among those solitary ones I might find a place that fit me well. Unreachable and beyond sympathy, I might join her, reveling in a freedom from concern for others, understanding at last that all is as it should be — not in the world, oh no, I could not so grandly generalize, but here, in my little neighborhood with its comings and goings, its small scandals and moonlight nights. Here all is, if not precisely well, at least in a kind of fluid balance. Family squabbles, cat fights, my own intermittent fits of depression — each seems the most important in the moment, but overall we know nothing here of trouble.

Here the afternoon is warm and I feel sleepy when I try to think. Down the street, the people in the old white Victorian are building a fence at the edge of their lawn. The street has grown busier this last year. One morning a few weeks ago I came across a dead cat still warm against the curb. Families with children and pets are well advised to build fences. It will be a low fence, I'm sure, with a gate and a friendly latch, not a lock. We are near the fire station; we are near the police station. I am not afraid to walk alone at night here; and if in those hours I choose to be nameless, as she is, surely there is no harm in it. If you called me then you might see in my face that wild inhuman look we see in Taffy's strange blue eyes; but not betrayal, for I would come, I think, if you called my name, though perhaps not just then, not that minute. Still, I would come back from that untamed place of enlightened distance the better for it. It's where I want to go, not to stay, but to come back wiser, to come back less destroyed by what you need of me.

The lilies are about to bloom, long spike stalks, fringed all the way up, and near the top, small oblong chartreuse buds, each morning more poised and swollen. I, on the other hand, feel empty, but it is a kind of dark emptiness which I sense contains something precious, could I but see into it. In last night's dream my eyes would not open. Now I see the stuffed trash cans along the wall and wait this morning's arrival of the weekly trash collectors, their gigantic truck groaning and clanking down the street like some Japanese cinema monster. The errant blackberry bushes push through along the fence, thick with white blossoms, many hard green pebbles of berries already showing. It's the same with the wild plums, their fruit, small and round and green, appears amid the leaves that feather each long branch, though their blossoms are gone since more than a month, and the leaves are dark. There's a lull in the inner world as external pressures mount.

Ratty is out and about, gnawing the inside of my mouth, thinking his beady-eyed thoughts, undermining me. He colors my view of things, dredges up old complaints, seduces me away from the comforting calm of the garden, the flowers, the warm afternoon light, urges me to run here and there, prevents me from settling in one place, concentrating on anything. This follows a difficult day yesterday when the world seemed an assault on my very center, my most primary commitments.

Jeff made me tea and toast and rubbed my shoulders. I'm tired. Is that what makes me vulnerable to Rat's intrusion? I want to sleep, a long uninterrupted sleep. Ratty is lonely. So lonely he can't allow himself to feel it. And he is frightened, too. The kind of fear we feel when we lose ourselves, the kind of fear that makes us hold on to everything tightly, the kind of fear that imagines there is not enough time or food or money or love—the scarcity model, an attitude of deprivation. A fear that there is no way out, that he is cornered and trapped. His little dark eyes are mistrustful. I recognize him as a presence not only in me, but in the world, a weary world, for that is when

Rat takes over, when we are weary and pressed.

The periwinkle-blue lobelia in my planter box virtually collapsed today in the blistering heat. Buddy lay on the floor for hours without moving; and I slept, a heavy sleep, unaware of traffic or the neighbors' voices, unaware of the sun that travelled west, flattening its glare against my bedroom blinds, a thick sleep, heat-drugged and bottomless and utterly apart, remembering nothing when I woke.

In the kitchen, the bouquet of wild flowers gathered at the dunes near the bay last night had wilted; the sprig of wild radish with its fragile lavender-veined petals drooped at the rim of the green glass vase. Only the yarrow stood straight on its stem. I opened the window wide. It was as hot outside as in, and the air did not stir. It's good that I'm alone, for Ratty is gnawing at me and this means I am the worst company. I need rest to protect me from Rat's twisted thinking, his narrow defensive scurrying mind, his beady-eyed suspicion and lack of empathy. What is he doing in my thoughts, in my mouth, chewing on the inside of my cheek, my lip? What is he hungry for? What is he afraid of?

It is only when I am tired like this that Rat gets a hold on me, only when I am so depleted that the world loses its color and a darkness gathers inside that absorbs all light, all subtle perception. It's not that Ratty doesn't notice detail, rather that he has no feeling for it. Detail to Ratty is information, data to be accumulated only because it might at some point be useful. He has no real concern besides survival, no compassion and no compunctions. He trusts no one, and he is not to be trusted.

"Me, me, me," he squeaks in his shrill aggressive little voice. His tiny teeth like so many small razor edges, sharp and dirty with insidiously invisible germs. He might carry the plague. I've got to isolate him, make a little wall around him, or a cage, then feed him something so he doesn't feel so desperate. I'd like to take him out someplace in a field near a woods and let him go. I wouldn't mind visiting him. Maybe that's what he really wants—to be set free in the wild where he belongs, where he cannot hurt anyone. He could scamper off then into the leaves and fallen logs at the meadow's rim, build himself a nest of sticks and dry grass and go to sleep. Meanwhile, I would rest better myself.

Now the morning sun floods the brown shingled wall and two east windows of the young red-haired man's apartment. It has moved sufficiently north to do this, in a matter of weeks! No more sharp shadow against the white wall of the young couple till after the Solstice. Against the shingles, the sun looks warmer. It will be another hot day. Already at six-thirty the streets hum with traffic. Last night's long satisfying dream has escaped, leaving only the sense of something healing from which I did not wish to wake; and I feel a trace of sadness to be entering the day, a tug back toward the fluffed pillows of my bed with its smooth white sheets. A single droplet tips the end of one bamboo leaf here in my planter box, just one amid all the others. Buddy observes from his post on the top step, now rises to sharpen his claws on the door mat.

I heard a scuttling, a sort of scraping, which at first I thought was Buddy on the far end of the porch, rummaging in the planter. Although it seemed odd for him to be doing this, I turned, searching for his dark shape there, but saw nothing in the half-moon light. Only then did I realize the sound came from below, from something moving on the ragged grass outside Jean and Terry's back door. Leonard's wife? I leaned back against the wall, feeling the cold of it, for it was chilly last night. From there I was able to make out a faint shape wavering in the dark below me. What was she doing? It was nearly midnight, and the moon to the west was a clear half-sphere, its edges softened by the high overcast. Then I saw that it was not Leonard's wife at all, but Jean, hanging the laundry, which this morning I see draped and pinned along the line. She continued about her domestic business, and I stood quietly in the shadow of my porch, retaining my privacy. It had been a long weekend, and this was a moment of welcome solitude. Also, it seemed an unlikely hour for conversation, dark as it was, late as it was, that moon hanging like a cold fruit high above the trees.

So it was not my wild revenant wandering in the yard, but Jean, who cooks and hangs laundry in the middle of the night. I saw Buddy, finally, near the bottom of the stairs, gliding silently along the walk-way, hesitating now and then, attentive in his feline way to each sound, to the other unseen cats of the neighborhood. Shortly there-after I slipped into the house, and before I closed the door, I heard Buddy's soft thumping up the stairs. Now here he is, crouched on the railing overlooking his territory, occasionally twitching an ear, turning his head, or lifting his tail in response to the various morning sounds, which are already accumulating around us at 7 a.m., as the last early bird-songs grow indistinct against the traffic of town. So far only the cats are stirring on the alley, though Jean and Terry's car is gone. Buddy hops down to sharpen his claws on the doormat, swishes his tail, and darts down the stairs. Sun brightens the brown shingles of the house next door, a low plane drones overhead; and the day readies itself for heat.

Leonard's wife has been quiet in her recent wanderings, or I have slept so deeply I've missed her appearances, for I've not seen or heard her for many nights now.

Below me, on the south side of the house, the little black dog is silent, invisible. Has something happened to him? The wild plum trees are thick with foliage and the tight pale greenness of the plums themselves has been supplanted by a golden orange and bright crim-son. Soon the fruit will fall, littering the path. I keep thinking about plum jam or chutney. It seems such a waste to let it fall and rot. But the wild plums are small, hardly larger than marbles, with slightly sour skins. We have a long harvest season, and it begins really with these plums, then the larger, dark red, Spanish plums, and on and on till autumn, when the apples and tomatoes come in. We take it for granted, all this fruit. It falls and feeds the birds, the ants, the worms.

My ex-husbands keep contacting me. If it isn't one, it's another. I can't tell you how disturbing it is—the one with his otter-eyes, which he turns to me so guilelessly, telling me about stream life in the Cas-cades, the Rio Grande cutthroat, with its large dark spots, that lives in the Pecos River, the insects inhabiting various types of canals, the wildflowers growing in the upper meadows of the Tetons, where we once traveled together. He has no idea what it does to me. He closes his eyes, squeezes them shut, trying to remember something, the name of a particular spiky magenta blossom, and I think of your face when we make love, that same shut tight moment at the point of no return.

I start remembering things I'd rather forget—the way his ears smelled, slightly acidic, like vinegar; the deftness of his hands as he tied two tiny red-orange feathers to a hook barely thicker than a medium-sized safety pin; how violent it seemed, hitting the head of a trout to kill it, how the color faded from their glistening bodies almost immediately, how watching their light grow dull always reminded me of the sudden shocking loss of luster on the fur of a kitten that died in my arms when I was nine. Buddy comes in, sniffs the ex-husband's shoes, climbs between us on the little floral couch, starts to curl up, but somehow doesn't, gets down, leaves, comes back, over and over. He can't quite relax, sensing the undercurrents—our familiarity, our ambivalence. I can't help wondering if Frank had lived what would have happened to us, if any of the others would have entered my life at all. Even you, my dearest, might have found the door closed.

Another husband, who gets on well with cats, of which we once had many, makes more noise than the biologist, and Buddy is less sure of him, winds through the room and out, then back, weaving his way through the furniture with each entrance and exit as if he needed the table, couch, chair, couch, table, etc., to protect himself. This husband is much smaller than the other, though noisier, and when I talk, miraculously he listens, only occasionally letting his eyes glaze over as he loses interest, a lapse for which I once poured orange juice on his head at the breakfast table.

This husband and I reached years ago such an understanding that our separation was quite mutual (un-like Frank's death, which I experienced rather like the wrenching apart of Siamese twins joined at the heart), but seeing him gives rise to certain questions, certain doubts. This husband also makes me laugh, no matter how sad I am, reminding me that after all, life is rather sad, and we have only laughter to console ourselves.

The biologist, who is otherwise quite reserved, delights in embarrassing me by indicating in various ways that he would like to resume our sexual relationship. I find it most disconcerting when I turn around to discover he has unzipped his pants to show me his charming accoutrements. He never fails to surprise me in this, and I have to laugh. The fact is, when a man makes me laugh, I can't help thinking of curling up in his arms. Laughter opens us, even more than tears.

I do not imagine Leonard's wife like me in these matters. She has separated herself in joining the wild ones. She might or might not enjoy sexual passion; but whatever she might choose, it would be what she wanted, nevermind the man; and she would never find her heart grown part of someone else's. Nor would she feel sad to see sadness in someone else's eyes, as I do, though she might well care and be concerned and be sweet. She might well think of fixing tea, or rubbing the feet, or tucking one in. But these are responses to passing sadness, not to the on-going underlying sadness that catches me by the throat and binds me.

This morning I feel my own sadness. It has been growing, opening slowly like a hauntingly scented flower I have no defense against and would root out if I could. But perhaps not. Perhaps like a bereaved child, I cling to the sadness because I am not yet ready to go on with my life alone, not yet whole enough to fully join another in the present. And I do not trust that without nostalgia I would find the past still with me.

Just as we do not want to forget the dead, and fear if we let go our memories, let go the grief of the fact that those memories are the past and gone now, we will have nothing, that the others will be gone forever and who we were gone with them. Yes, that the self we were will vanish, leaving only an abyss behind us, only a deep absence, a nothingness we fall back into. So ultimately it is my own annihilation I defend against. And this is what the husbands felt; there was a way I held myself apart. And this is what Rat has tried to protect me from, this sadness, which is also the precious metal I must mine.

I know that I am not who I was, that I am constantly changing and shifting like sand in the sea, that there is only the present, only now. Yet it is as if I have never caught up with myself. Life speeds by so fast, I'm always behind, still trying to comprehend what happened years ago—like a cat licking a wound to try to heal it. And they do, usually, better than a vet can; but it takes time. And anyway, how far can I carry this analogy? After all, I have no visible wounds; and my tongue is not antiseptic, which is a marvelous thing about cats, those antiseptic tongues.

Buddy has gone off to snack, and it's gotten late. They're hammering down in the drive behind the house where the landlord is having a deck put in. Oh yes, and a real garden. Leonard's wife will love that!

It does confuse me, though, seeing the husbands. And afterward I dream strange dreams. Last night I tried merely to close the door quietly. I worked on this, closing the door over and over in the dream. But when the dream men came looking for me, the doors I had to close were a different kind, and all my practice was for naught.

At ten p.m., Terry was out taking in the laundry as I sat quietly on the porch. I saw the leaf shadows moving in moonlight against the white wall, the moon a crisp semi-sphere, sharp-edged as a slice in the black sky. I went to bed, thinking of Lorca. The night chill was deep and sank into my shoulders as I slept, finally waking me before dawn. Then I slept again. This morning no visible changes in the lily buds. Fog. The birds quiet, still tucked in, waiting for the sun. Now Buddy zooms downstairs to investigate a rustling in the garden.

There's something about the morning light slipping from dawn to sun-up, the edges of the rising sun muted with mist that clears gradually, first condensing above the laguna, before it puddles close to the ground and then is gone. It's best to water the garden then, so the moisture sinks, for the days are hot; and the flowers are happiest early, eager faces lifted, where as later the heat will exhaust them. For the moment, a stillness pervades the yards and the alley. But even now, the business of the day thickens, gathering to blot out dreams and the privacy of darkness. Leonard's wife, of course, has vanished.

Buddy swishes his tail, like a fin, topaz eyes wide and alert to the increasing activity of daylight. Once again the shadows on the white wall of the neighbor's house grow sharp and perfect as the sun begins its slow trek south. Buddy watches from the porch as the black cat next door sniffs around the garbage cans like an errant doppelganger, as if the two were reflections released from one another in some peculiar violation of the laws of matter. Jean's laundry hangs on the line, the towels and sheets inert, shirts and trousers poised for the rescue of a body. Expectation is inherent in the morning hours, the neighborhood begins to breathe, releasing the peace of night with a sigh, admitting to itself the thrust of yet another day. Always I want to go on sleeping. Always I am glad to have risen early, grateful for the transition these early hours provide.

The fog rolled in last night after two days of sweltering heat. Everything is very still inside the house. Ratty gnaws at the inside of my lip and thinks muddled calculating thoughts: how to protect myself, to keep things nice so everyone is happy and uncritical of me. But Ratty is exposed now. What would happen if I didn't listen to him? I'd have more fun, be more flexible, less defensive. I'd feel the fear of displeasing, the fear of not being able to control, to keep my distance. And I like to keep my distance. I suppose because I have such trouble doing it. It seems so easy to fall into closeness, to feel what others feel, to drown in their needs for attention.

I think the second husband was a relief because he asked so little of me, only that I be there, a presence in the house, like television, but even less, since I need not have spoken much—more like the bed or the couch or a comfortable chair, or, yes, a houseplant! Something living and breathing, but speechless and undemanding. No, this is unfair. It's just that I felt invisible and mute. Still, at first I liked it that I didn't have to be his audience, that he had so little to say to me. In the end, though, I disappointed all of them with my own retreats, my psychic absenteeism. I ran myself ragged with work and there was nothing left but Ratty, backed into a corner, ready to show his teeth when all else failed.

I watered early today, knowing it would be hot, a dry heat that parches plant and animal alike, air against which women guard themselves with protective lotions, dark glasses, and broad-brimmed hats. I watered early, noting at last the lilies have bloomed, crisp white trumpets heralding the end of summer, tall and regal above the pedestrian white alyssum, red geraniums, and pink petunias.

The fact is I am haunted, not only by the dead, but by the living, and not solely by their will. I see this now. Last night I dreamed of you. But in the dream you got mixed up with Frank. You were picking up divorce papers from your last marriage in Nevada, where Frank died. I woke to the fuzzy grey of street-lamp light diffused by fog, alone in my bed, save for Buddy curled at my feet, the approach of dawn signaled by the prehistoric rasping of the street cleaner. I closed the window and returned to bed. Buddy shifted slightly on the blankets and stretched out his long slender forelegs, extending and then retracing his claws again as he relaxed.

Later this morning it came to me that I might be afraid to really love you. But that sounds melodramatic. I'm afraid because I don't know how to stand up to your moods. I don't know how to stop you when you bully me. And you don't give a fig about being reasonable. So I grow cautious and secretive. Rat's way. He estimates the chances for escape, calculates a detour, sits on the telephone so I can't answer it. Muteness again. No wonder Leonard's wife enjoys so much her drifting and wandering. She has no quarrel with the confining images of wife, mother, or neighbor now. What does she care how she is remembered? She does as she pleases, with no concern whatever for the opinions of others.

The sun has risen above the branches of the pine to the southeast and leans warmly on my shoulder as I sit near the window. The silver roof of the feed store on the other side of Main Street flares white against its backdrop of oaks; and the two plexiglass skylights on the library roof glisten like cataract-filmed eyes. My own eyes tug to go out of focus. I surrender for a moment and thought ceases. Neighborhood activity and street sounds form a soft net of noises, comforting in my momentary lack of concentration. No birds, but the whirred thrumming of a Volkswagen starting up, further off a truck rumbling north, the hammering of carpenters down the block, the buzz of a skill saw—all this against the low continuous waves of traffic like a white noise in this white-hot day where not a leaf moves on the poised tree-lined horizon.

The eyes of my sister's painting are somehow accusatory. The house needs cleaning, dust like a thin garment across the wood floor. I drift, and a state near sleep lures me. I resist simply because the solitude is precious. Such moments as this—with no one waiting, no one on earth at this moment knowing just exactly where I am or what I am doing—are a luxury. And where is she, Leonard's wife? She understands what you cannot, my dearest, my sweet enslaver. She understands the joy of being lost to all the world, as I do, for just a little while.

III

I wanted to tell you about the jasmine, the sky spread with pale shell-pink and ecru clouds, the half-moon hung for all the world as if it were no more than that piece of itself in the blue evening sky. Because it is a warm evening, I sit outside to feel the air as soft as breath on my bare arms. Today you kissed my backbone where my shirt pulled up when I bent to pick a pin up off the floor. So I stayed bent and let you kiss me up my spine and back down. The smell of jasmine envelopes me, is part of the air in a way that cannot be separated from it. And that moon! I understand completely how certain one could be that it grows and then shrinks into darkness, rhythmically repeating this process, for if I did not know it, I would never believe that a whole moon is up there now, when I can see clear through that absent half, see the blue sky darkening into twilight.

On the street, the traffic zooms past with short spells of silence between, though it's nearly nine o'clock on a weeknight. Summer keeps us up, keeps us out; even the children ride their bikes till dark. We are just past the equinox, and these warm days are the longest we'll see as we slide now through the deeper heat of July and August, toward the autumn equinox.

The pale shell-pink has spread wider and smears the whole of the southern sky—brighter now, deeper pink, nearing flamingo, and spread like icing, as if one should sweep a hand up to catch it on a fingertip and suck. As if the sky were a sweetness so very near, and yet this is illusion, as it is illusion that the moon is not always whole and present though not always visible. Truth requires faith, faith in returnings after departures, faith in the rhythmic essence of nature. While at the same time, I must have faith in the wholeness of things, of the world and of myself.

People come and go from the neighborhood, from below me, where Jean is packing to leave and a new family will be moving in, from the old apartment where once Jim lived and now the young woman puts flowers on the table, from the apartment where now the young couple have taken the curtains down and put up Japanese blinds. Only Taffy remains, prowling about in his proprietary way, permanently puzzled and angry.

One night when the moon was full, you knocked on my door, and when I let you in, you held me hard against you. I felt as full as the moon, a fullness to bursting, as if I would never wane, as if giving would only bring more fullness, like the suckled breast that drops more milk, a flood of milk, unending if it is only sucked upon. Heart to heart we pressed, and desire seemed to me then only the spilling over of milk, of a fullness that could not be contained. I did not see that desire might come from the wound of loss, of emptiness. Perhaps this is a lie, perhaps it was my wound I loved in you and wanted to heal, an old emptiness I wanted once and for all to fill. I did not see that full moon as the same moon which was also a half-moon, a quarter moon, a dark moon. Was it self-deception then? A willful blindness? There was such joy in our wanting, I did not bear in mind the lesson of the moon's waning.

For am I not also, like the moon, both light and dark, both full and not full? And did I not also long to be filled as I wanted to fill you? Did I not long to feel your fullness in me, driving into my open place, my dark place, my empty room? Did I not say: yes, I want you, please, come? —as if I would never have enough?

I could breathe this jasmine scented air and never get enough, though it suffuses my lungs with sweetness. Its season will wane, its blossoms fade; winter follows summer ad infinitum. I could almost lick this sky, almost taste it on my tongue, as you might lick the bones of my back, my thigh, the salt of my skin, your mouth a hollow that gives and takes.

Wind slaps the outdoor blind against the porch rail, and behind the horizontal slats the sun peers through the fog like a blank white eye. Across town, I hear the children at the swimming pool, though it hardly seems warm enough today. Buddy meanders through the bushes along the alley, appearing and disappearing from view. The fog clings to the landscape, cool and sticky as cotton candy. Saw Taffy out here last night. He's recovering quite nicely from his spring molt and looks generally rather respectable these days. I think Ann has been putting food out for him.

Buddy snoozes, having flattened himself against me lengthwise, head on my knees, rump against my stomach, wisely fitting himself so that only his errant tail drapes its tip in a black hook against the blue upholstery of my special chair, the one he is not allowed to set foot upon. The mid-day overcast has dropped to the ground level in a fine mist that stretches across the laguna to the eastern hills. The wind bullies its way through the trees in long intermittent shushes.

Last night, near midnight, under the near-full moon, Jean hung her laundry again. I had been asleep and was wakened by the spin cycle of her washing machine, which shakes the timbers of the house so that in my bed I feel the floor shudder in the semblance of an earthquake, which is what I thought it was the first two or three times it happened. I even asked people the next day if they had felt the earthquake, receiving in response a series of blank stares, because of course I persisted, certain there had been one, asking not one or two people, but possibly five or six. I had gone through this entire routine several times before one afternoon when I had a record on. I heard the washer downstairs, and eventually a disruptive vibrating and simultaneous distortion of Handel's *Water Music,* which correlated with the washing machine's activity—the spin cycle to be precise. "Oh yes," Jean said when I asked her about it, "the machine is out of balance. Terry's tried to fix it, but it's still not right." Somehow the shuddering remains most noticeable from my bedroom, and since Jean often does laundry at the unlikely hours between ten and midnight, I often wake, as I did last night, to the disconcerting sensation of the house shivering spasmodically.

I get up, put on my robe, and wander out to the porch to look at the moon. Last night, there was Jean, pinning clothes to the line. She must have done her whites, because the row of towels, sheets, shirts and socks gleamed against the dark garden in the light of the growing moon like ice floating in a night sea. I had thought I heard Leonard's wife at the pond earlier, but she was nowhere to be seen. Still, I had the distinct feeling she had been there, watching Jean hang the laundry, shaking her head, no doubt, her wild hair rippling as she reveled in her liberty. No laundry for her to hang! No washing in the middle of the night for her! Only her feral wanderings, her amusement over once taking everything so seriously. When she shakes her head like that, half disbelieving, it is herself she remembers, how it was when she too washed clothes at midnight and fell finally to bed, so tired she slept right through Leonard's coughing and muttering.

On a blistering morning, the heat swelling in every enclosed and pocketed place, cars already ovens along the street at 8 a.m., a peculiar stillness holds us, an odd sense of suspension. At breakfast on Main Street we have omlettes, whole wheat toast with jam, and coffee. We haven't heard the news. Not until your friend coaching swimming at the park pool meets you at the fence. And by the time I join the two of you, crossing the hot asphalt parking lot, passing the bleachers, he is finishing the story.

"Who was it?" I ask. "What happened?"

Now in the afternoon shade, the hum of bees part of the air itself, the flawless blue sky, I imagine for a moment the imprint of such immobilizing heat, how it suits the state of shock and disbelief of family and friends, even myself, though I had never met her. Nothing like this has happened here before. We are not innured to such events as they are in New York or Chicago or Memphis. We are not prepared. We do not understand.

"Does this mean," I ask you later, "that I shouldn't walk alone at night anymore?" I who have always felt so safe, and taken such pleasure in that sense of safety, that trust in my community, I who have walked the three blocks from my house to where it happened many times at night, often late.

"I don't know," you answer. But I am not satisfied. I miss a sense of your concern. I wonder if you are angry at me and hardly know it yourself. I've felt it before. I've watched the pattern unfold—first a seeming lack of interest, then the snide remarks, the growing edge of sarcasm, then the accusations. I do not want to repeat the process again. We walk home apart from each other, a distance between us which you do not seem to notice, but I brood upon it. It feels as wide as the continent.

"I haven't told the children yet," Jean says. She and Terry are moving to a new house, and she is packing, folding small sweaters, jackets, and dresses, putting them in boxes. She looks up at me. "Leah saw it," she says.

"Saw what?" Susie wants to know, and Jean pauses before she turns to answer.

"A woman was killed last night. Murdered."

I want to know what time it happened. I have to know. If it was late, that will tell me something I already understand about violence, about danger. But it happened just before dark. If something like this can happen in a public place, at an hour when ordinary people presume themselves safe, when are we ever safe?

When we left the park, we went there, where it happened, because you had to mail a letter. I waited for you. It was nearly noon. Everything looked the same. Four children sat with a box of kittens outside the main doors of the Post Office. The kittens, they told me, were free. For a moment I forgot a woman had been knifed through the neck a few yards away little more than twelve hours earlier.

What does it mean to lose one of ourselves like that?

Down the street, the pickets for the fence have not been touched, as if in tacit correspondence with this suspended state.

At your house, you putter in the kitchen. You thank me for the roses I put on your desk and bring me a glass of water. You are not thinking of her now. But I am a woman, and women see things differently. We know we are all potential victims. I have trusted my intuition and my instincts all my life. Now what can I trust? It could have been me. It could have been my best friend, or your friend's wife. I hear the bees in the hedge of honeysuckle. In this heat their buzzing seems ominous. Last night I dreamed I had been shot. The bullet was inside me. "You have to fix me," I told my assailant, "because we can't live without each other."

I do not know what the dream means, but I think it has to do with all of us. Some old quarrel has to be resolved. Something to do with male and female. I lean back, feeling the dampness under my arms, at the back of my neck. I close my eyes, and the husbands parade past, their faces full of sadness and accusations. "Guilty," they pronounce, turning away from me. I know I should repent, ask forgiveness, but what is it I have done exactly? The clock on the wall in the courtroom has stopped. Nothing can go on until I remember my crime.

The moon was full last night. The Moon of the Dry Grass, the August moon. It shone on the white wall of the young couple's apartment, but the wall did not gleam silver as you might expect. No, it gleamed such a golden apricot that I glanced back to see if a strange cloud had crossed the moon; but there was nothing.

Buddy climbed out onto the lattice above the deck being built where Jean used to hang her laundry. In the moonlight, his black fur glistened. I saw him swish his tail once, then several times, before he stopped and crouched so still he all but disappeared in the dark. Then I heard a rustling and saw Taffy emerge from the bushes, Leonard's wife behind him. She stepped up onto the new deck and spent some moments examining the lattice and the upright timbers of the new fence.

Taffy kept pace with her, rubbing back and forth against her legs. His long coat seemed to shiver like pale flame in the moonlight, while on the planks of the deck his shadow moved with him like a sticky dark pool. It was odd watching the two of them move slowly around the construction site, she stepping gingerly over a stack of 2 × 4s here, a tool box there. Buddy and I had been watching quite a while before I realized the really odd thing was that Leonard's wife cast no shadow. No matter how she stood in the moonlight, no darkness followed or preceded her as it did Taffy. I suppose everyone knows a ghost casts no shadow, but I had never thought about it.

This morning it occurred to me the apricot light on the side of the apartment last night might have been from the fire burning north of here. Earlier in the afternoon the sky held a long brownish-orange fog-like cloud, which I recognized then must be smoke, though the fire is many miles away. I keep thinking about it, knowing while my life goes on as usual, a completely different reality exists—a world of dense smoke and blazing heat, of forty-pound water packs carried on the backs of fire-fighters, of animals running, their fur in flames, trees igniting with an initial explosive fireworks. Frank died in such a fire, pinned under a great log that rolled downhill out of the inferno, coming to rest in a hearth atop his body. There was nothing I could do, nothing anyone could do. For three days the fire swept steadily through the forests and meadows, leaping the fire-retardant laid down in long swaths by Forestry planes. There was no stopping it. It burned a month in the roots underground, flaring from cave-ins. The whole earth was ash, ankle-deep and deeper in places, like a filthy snow. Every living thing was charred.

Sometimes I dream of fire—fire licking the sky as it races through the grass, explodes in the trees. In the dream, Frank is working just ahead of me, swinging and scraping the earth with his mattocks to make a break. It's as if I have a zoom lens and can see up close, though it's a long way and there are several others working between us. A bandana covers his nose and mouth. Above it, his face is streaked with dirt and smoke and sweat. He looks down at the clumsy fangs of the mattocks pumping rhythmically with each stroke as he plunges the blade-side through the mat of grass over and over into the earth beneath, cutting, tearing away and scraping back the grass to expose the raw dirt. I can see all this in an instant. I know what is going

to happen next, and I want to warn him. "Frank!" I scream.
"Frank!" But the roar of the fire drowns my voice and he doesn't hear
me. He doesn't hear me.

Last night I dreamed of fire racing across a grassy plain, bursting
beside me and behind me so there was nowhere to go, no place that
wasn't burning. Horses ran from the wave of fire, their manes aflame.
And then you came to lead me to an earthen house the fire swept right
over, leaving us safe in a sea of ash. I woke then and reached for you,
but you my dear, my knife, my rock, my bridge, my blanket, my har-
bor, you were not there.

They've picked up a suspect in the murder case—her ex-
husband, the man she divorced twenty-nine years ago, when she was
eighteen. It's hard to believe someone could hold that kind of grudge.
But he fits the description of witnesses. At least that makes some
sense, if murder ever makes sense, which it doesn't. And though it
seems strange, more than one of the neighbors, like myself, has
breathed a certain sigh of relief at the probability that he's the killer.
How much worse to think it could have been a random murder, with-
out the particularities of any kind of relationship. Which is truly more
terrifying, attack by a stranger, or attack by someone you know well?
Most murders are committed by husbands who kill their wives. Did he
try to kill her all those years ago, or only dream of it till now? What
happened between them that could lead to this?

Most often you know your assailant, how he brushes his teeth,
the hours he sleeps and how deeply, what he eats for breakfast, his
footsteps, his voice in the dark. You would know him anywhere. He
has touched you many times. You are bound to one another in ways
no divorce proceeding, later marriage, or separation can alter.

The details form a picture, a story, a shared life, and while these
details may not in themselves seem significant, they speak of the level
of intimacy once shared between two people who no longer see one an-
other; there is something deeply disturbing and unnatural about this.
We weren't meant to share such closeness and survive it to go so far
our separate ways. This crazy ex-husband, who drove west from out-
of-state and stabbed his ex-wife to death in mere moments had had

years to seethe and simmer. Maybe he couldn't stand her knowing how many minutes he took to brush his teeth. Maybe he blamed her for his financial ruin.

I'm not nearly so unnerved when I drive past the Post Office now; and I've resumed my night walks. Down the street they're back at work on the fence. They've painted the framing white, and they're ready to nail up the pickets.

Have I had a husband who might wish me dead? I don't think so, but one might, in a moment of frustration, have wanted to kill me. It is possible. If I turned away in an argument and refused to speak. Or if I spoke in anger, laying bare some fragile aspect of character, some old wound, if I shamed him—who knows? My second husband probably wanted to kill me—for a moment at least—when I poured orange juice on his head. I jumped from my chair and ran before he could grab me. Oh yes, I was afraid. I knew I had gone too far. But he got over it.

I brush my teeth so long sometimes anyone thinking about it would wonder if I'm obsessive, which my sister used to call me. I think if anyone ever wanted to kill me, it was she; and we shared an intimacy of unmatched duration in my life—shared the same room for seventeen years. How one brushes one's teeth is the kind of detail one might want kept private. Maybe her ex-husband imagined she told her present husband all about him, and the thought drove him mad. I've kept certain things to myself for years. We all have our secrets. Even you, the other day, asked me if I had looked in your drawer. "You might find my secrets," you said, with a mock scowl. I would have joked then: "What secrets," I might have said, "girlie magazines?" But you would have been insulted. Whereas, having actually made such a discovery, once with one of the husbands who hid his collection, and later with another husband whose collection was not a secret but was still a shock, I have come to some terms with the matter; though to be honest, I'm relieved that you do not collect pornography.

When I got home there was a party going on across the alley. Reggae music, loud and pulsing in the evening air, voices and laughter, and Leonard's wife swaying gently in the shadows. She and Leonard never danced. There wasn't time. And anyway, why would he want to dance? Now she can dance all she wants, without a partner! Dead women don't need partners to dance. She enjoys the liveliness of the present neighborhood, never a dull moment, and no Leonard looking over her shoulder, criticizing her, always dissatisfied. "To die," she says softly, "is to be reborn."

It doesn't matter to the murdered woman. She is dead, like Leonard's wife, and now she knows the secret of release. Now she is free of both husbands, the first and the second. She drifts around the parking lot by the Post Office where she was killed, marveling that she no longer has any place in particular to go, no one waiting for her to come home with the shopping. She is sympathetic still to the ones left behind. After all, it hasn't been long. They haven't even got the stone up yet. But already she begins to enjoy herself, floating about these warm Indian Summer nights. And though they call her name, she hesitates only a moment before she shakes off the memory and surrenders herself to air. "Oh," she cries delightedly as she floats over my garden, "the lilies! There's so much I've missed!" For there they are, luminous and gleaming in the dark, their perfume all around us.

The music has stopped. It's Sunday night, and the party is over. You have gone home, returning to your own kind of darkness. Miles away you sit in your own garden and smoke another cigarette. What does it matter, the copper taste in your mouth, you're not going to kiss me. You watch the moon hunched over the redwoods. The flowers and herbs we planted are motionless. Only your mind travels back and forth in its inescapable night.

Once you kissed the bones of my spine and whispered, "You're beautiful." My spine remembers those kisses. Maybe someone else will kiss each vertebra and whisper to me and lick the inside of my thigh. The nights are warm, the moon just new, and dancing is in my back, in my legs, in my arms and my neck, with or without a partner. I shall be a silver snake. I shall twin myself and dance with the mirror. Spine to spine, cool glass, a reflection of pleasure, so I know that I am here. This is not loneliness. This is not sorrow.

Love spills over like a cool spring onto thirsty earth. All around things sprout, greenery pushes up through gravel. I pulled weeds from the gravel steps; they came up again. Why pull them? Why stop their reclamation of what is theirs? I too shall reclaim myself. My body will be mine again; my heart will belong to me again. How foolish all that struggle to share my life, as if it were a burden. But that is not what I felt.

I felt only the burden of so much ungiven, of pleasures unshared, kisses unkissed. Now I have given those kisses. I have worn myself out with giving. Is it so bad? Is it so terrible, this empty place? Is it not peaceful at last? Is there not joy in this solitude, even a sense of wholeness? As the night reclaims its silence when the music stops, as the weeds reclaim what was theirs before we dug the steps and spread the gravel, why should I not allow solitude to reclaim me with its stillness? All this tumultous loving has spent itself, all the promises and pledges and effort to understand. What loss is there really? I am not even weary.

If I let go, I float free. I no longer answer to you. I come and go where I will, nameless even unto myself. And this is good, for the nameless shall be everchanging and eternal. Why name those birds that sing at night whose names I longed to know? They might be any birds, invisible in the dark. They might be any color, all color, even as I am any color, all color, no color at all, perhaps black, like Buddy, who comes to the window at night and cannot be seen but for his topaz eyes.

Without you to shape my body with your touch, it is only my body. Apart from you, my love, my dear one, my captor, apart from you my body takes the shape I bestow upon myself. This skin, I take it upon myself. How could I have abandoned it to you for so long.

Jean and Terry and the kids are gone. Below me a forgotten quiet has returned. I am truly alone in a vacant house; inside, I am me and not me, but something new, all embracing, large and private. Voices of the past rise and fall through the silence of the present—Leonard's wife weeping, Leonard coughing, his son's voices lifting in eternal argument, Mary sighing in her sleep, Terry ranting at midnight about the state of the world, children of all ages running through the rooms laughing. The ghost of Leonard's wife passes through the door, runs her hand along the top of the wainscoting as she glides from room to room, remembering. She pauses, listens, shakes her head and smiles. Gone. Changed. And then her own laughter ripples through the dark house and out into the garden.

The yellow baby mums are almost the very same yellow as my tea cup, the cup that rests on the end table beside the couch. The yellow mums in their vase beside the cup are withering, the blossoms browning slightly from the center out, the stems, visible through the clear glass, swollen and soggy, tinging the water a yellow-brown, releasing a faint smell of decay. They ought to be thrown out. But I don't want to get up.

Buddy is on my lap, purring nicely, and I really couldn't think of disturbing him. He stretches his front leg out over my left arm, immobilizing it. I allow this restriction, though it means I can no longer reach my cup, because he is soft and warm and seems so happy plumped on my lap and purring. After all, I encouraged him to come out here into the living room. He might well have stayed where he was, on the desk, under the drafting lamp, snoozing in the heat of its sixty watt bulb, if I hadn't given him a pat and said, "Come on," when I left the room.

It's dark out, a drizzly night, and not the sort of evening he would like to go out into. I reach my right hand across and manage to capture the yellow cup for a sip of the little remaining tea. Buddy extends his other foreleg out beside the first, and I manage during his readjustment to extract my left arm.

Really, I'd rather just surrender. Let the cat sleep, let the tea get cold, let the mums wither and rot. I'd just as soon lean back and go to sleep myself. It's getting late. I'll just have a little nap before bed. How you laughed the first time I said that!

Buddy swishes his tail, and I think how like a snake that black tail is. How wicked and seductive. If only I didn't have to work tomorrow. If only tomorrow were Sunday and the paper were being delivered, and one could simply lie in bed with tea and the *Literary Review!* "Ah, that would be heaven, wouldn't it, pal," I say to Buddy, and I give him a scratch behind the ears.

This last full moon I noticed something I had never been aware of before. When the moon is full, the crickets sing deep into the night, until the moon sets. I take this as an indication of extensive celebration, celebration far beyond my limited perception. I bet every full moon there's a great to-do all over the earth, which we with our concrete freeway lives mostly miss. Surely the crickets who exhaust themselves singing all night are not the only creatures engaged in instinctive ecstatic rites. Surely all animals in nests and burrows and dens are similarly moved. Surely the rabbits have convocations, twitching their long ears, and the deer, too.

I know the coyotes sing, for I have heard them more than once, their chorus rising and falling and rising again in waves of joyous kinship. Though I have never observed it, certainly the mice must scurry about with special zest, and the owls—unquestionably the owls have a larger palate from which to select their supper, and this must be cause for a certain excitement.

We strolled the shoreline, you and I, high on the cool sand, for the moon had pulled the sea up to make a series of salty lakes and inlets all along the beach. We listened to the bay buoys, and watched their lights flick on and off, watched the fishermen, too, in their grand little boats, the rigging, a dark and delicate dance against the moonlit water.

Sometimes I sense a longing in you, and I think of your fishing years, days and nights in the Straits of Juan de Fuca, in the cold and wet of those seas. It could have been your life, and we would not have met, would not be walking here under the full moon. Frank might have lived and been with me now.

The boats offshore turn on the axis of their anchors, drifting in the current, their profiles shifting against the shining water. You imagine the crew, the interior cabin, the engine, the slow billow of nets underwater. You smell the hot coffee, feel the easy rocking, hear the soft resonant slap of water against the hull. We gaze seaward, and I am the woman waiting on land, you are the man at sea. I feel the sand, a silver dampness against my feet, while your eyes scan the shimmering horizon, knees flexed for the roll of the deck under you.

At last we turn back. We have this life now, together. Something closes behind us. Ahead a door opens, another path unfolds. And there are moments for each of us when we feel the fear of wild mustangs herded down narrowing canyons, who sense there is no going back, who sense the trap ahead, the inescapable end toward which they thunder.

It seems to me now perfectly right that I should love you, who remind me of my uncles and of my father. Your eyes are very like my father's, although I've never told you this; and the way you look aside at me, wickedly raising one eyebrow, is like him, too. Like a photograph my mother has of him taken years ago when he was just about your age. And your legs are like his, thickly muscled and pale and adjusted to the slanting rhythms of decks at sea. It seems perfectly right that she should have loved such a man, who reminded her of her brothers, her own father, for how else shall we persist in this life which over time leaves us so alone, bereft of family, of the childhood intimacy we take for granted till it's gone? The salty smell of your skin resembles that of my kindred, close packed in the old Ford, coming home from the beach, sticky and hot in the back seat, sand in our shoes, our hair, our bathing suits. His legs, my father's legs. And when you hold me, I feel enveloped in your body, smooth skin, a veneer of softness, and hard solid muscle and heavy bone beneath, so it is like being held by the world somehow, by earth and fire both at once.

What else could be so urgent as this need for a face that keeps us company over the years as we change? We need it more urgently than ever as the appearance of our lives grows more separate from our roots, as the landscape changes, shopping centers springing from familiar fields, condos from old farmhouses, tourist developments from fishing villages. Why should it be a surprise that we need each other, or that we want more than a fleeting affair? Why not hold fast to what we've found, to stave off the rest, at least while we can? And so I cling to the small repetitions of my daily life as I feel myself float, ephemeral upon the world—morning sunlight gleaming silver off the aluminum screens on the neighbor's window, the secret hope that I might be pregnant with your child, a child who would be my father, or my grandmother, or my sister all over again in a gesture, or laugh, a certain inflection—to sustain the pattern begun before I was born.

And the others? The ones who grew angry or disappointed and went away? Why should they not also want to return, to hold on to even the fragments of what they thought they'd found in me, though this cannot be, though they must let go, even as I must let them go? Frank is so far away now, gone forever. He will not return here, though I have wished it and have fooled myself with faces like his own, his clear eyes, his thick dark hair. His hands were my mother's hands, strong and fine and competent, his language an echo of hers, an educated mix of scientific fact and a poet's romance.

His temper, too, was like hers, quick and cutting and slow to fade. He was another kind of twin. He could have been my brother. I held him between me and the multitude. I lived behind him while I lay beside him. Such a life could not go on, would have to come finally to crisis.

After his death, no wonder I held myself apart so the others could not reach me, no wonder I have feared you, too, would go—Ratty's fear, cold and disembodying. But you do not go. Or rather, you do not let me go. You are not so polite, not so respectful, not so Victorian and aristocratic in your passion. You are right to be angry and right to storm around growling and roaring. How else shall I learn not to abandon you, since in my old fear, I see you leaving, joining with the others in their accusations and departure.

Buddy crouches on the sill of the open window, silhouetted against the mottled clouds; his whiskers are lines drawn with black ink. And I sit below him on the floor, feet propped against the edge of the bathtub, both of us watching the sky, the lights of town, passing cars, people. We watch together, silent for the most part, though occasionally I speak, murmuring to him. He flicks his ear back. This is how he listens. And I listen to Bartok.

From the other room, the notes rise and fall in a rush, like water. I listen, and I watch, and I think random flickering thoughts while the record plays. Somewhere near the end of Side 1, as I stare absently at the corner of the shower where the tile meets the porcelain, I feel an inner stopping. No more scattered thoughts. A moment of utter calm, so I laugh out loud.

Oh the roundness, the perfection of circularity, of repetition, which we recognize finally only because it is broken. Intersecting, overlapping rhythms enfold us. This is our world, our life. And it is our fear that calls for fixity, for the certainty of the eternal. Yet this too we are granted over time. And if time could be seen in its wholeness, all wounds would be healed, all doubts allayed. This is a love story. It ends with each word, and it never ends, for all endings are arbitrary.

I will always love you. I will want you to call my name, though you cannot name me. I will rise in the dawn and be less than myself, something greater left behind in the dark. It will take the night to make me visible. And so we love pieces of each other. To love more is to love the mystery, the nameless, that which we cannot hold onto.

If Leonard could have loved her wholly, if he could have held in his heart what could not be possessed, perhaps he would be with her now, and she would not drift from hedge to pond to lilac, the wraith that she is. Or I might be mistaken. Perhaps it is our true nature to be alone and learn to rejoice in that solitude, to know we are bound together through it, above it, beyond it. Always.

❧

EILEEN'S DAUGHTER

EILEEN'S DAUGHTER

MARLA STARED OUT THE WINDOW of the unfamiliar room watching dusk settle in the L.A. basin. "Well, Momma, here we are," she thought. Down the hall the cocktail party gathered momentum. She turned and caught her image in the mirror, her skin glowing faintly against the black sleeveless dress. It surprised her. She still expected to see little Marla, with stringy hair and bony elbows. She smiled to herself and stepped around the bed to move closer to the mirror. It was then she saw the gloves, their dark cuffs extending from the pocket of a suede coat lying in the pile of coats on the big double bed.

"Momma," Marla said the last time she had seen her mother, "I'm going to California." She had waited for the news to sink in, waited for some response. But there had been none. Her mother had not moved. Her face remained expressionless, eyes fixed on a distance beyond what Marla could measure.

"Momma," Marla reached over then and tentatively touched her mother's arm, "did you hear me? Want to come with me, Momma?"

Her mother had not moved at all during the entire visit. Nor had she spoken or moved on Marla's preceeding visit.

"Don't you want to see the ocean, Momma?" Marla whispered.

Marla reached for the gloves. Her hand slid easily through the slit in the soft suede, into the pocket of the coat as she lifted it. She followed the tongue of dark leather into the pocket where her fingers had just entwined with those of the gloves when she heard a noise in the hall. She froze.

"Go ahead, do it. I dare you! I dare you!"

They stared at each other. Marla's face was chalk white. She stood stiffly, hands clenched at her sides. Joanne stood opposite her, chin jutting out and head tilting upward slightly in challenge. She leaned toward Marla. Marla's mouth jerked sideways, twitching, but she did not cry. She had watched Joanne cross the bridge, walking slowly along the slippery stone railing, her arms out like wings for balance, while the current tore through the jagged gorge below, splashing a continuous mist up to meet the intermittent rain. Now it was Marla's turn.

"I dare you." Joanne leaned still closer to her sister, her lips pulled back. "Scaredy-cat," she hissed.

"I don't have to listen to you." Marla turned away, tramping through the wet leaves beside the bridge, her plaid skirt hanging where the hem was soaked.

"Scaredy-cat, scaredy-cat," Joanne called after her.

Marla covered her ears with her hands. "I'm not listening," she yelled over Joanne's voice and began to sing loudly to herself.

"Marla's a scaredy-cat," Joanne continued, "Marla's a scaredy-cat."

"I am not!" Marla stopped walking, dwarfed against the mountains behind her and the turmoil of the dark shifting clouds. "I am not," she screamed. "I am not. I am not."

But Joanne kept calling.

"Shut up, just shut up! I hate you. Leave me alone!"

Joanne continued chanting.

The great black clouds opened with a roll of thunder that drummed out their voices and the two girls were soaked in minutes by the downpour. Marla's sandy hair flattened against her head. Tears streamed down her cheeks, warm and salty at the corner of her mouth mixed with the cold rain on her face, a child's face, wet and slick, her mouth twisted and open.

Joanne moved in then. She moved in close, till her face was almost touching Marla's, and when she spoke her voice was low and even. "You think I care how you feel? You dummy. I hate you more. I've always hated you. You're stupid and ugly. You look like him. She doesn't love you either. She loves me. I can't stand being around you. I hate sleeping in the same room with you. You should just go away."

It had stopped raining when Marla paused by the maples at the edge of the woods. Beyond her lay the meadow—grass thick with rain, a vivid green. She stood beneath the branches which were the last shelter before the open meadow. Above her the yellow leaves chattered in the wind. A single leaf torn loose sailed out over the clearing. The road was across the meadow. Marla could feel the dampness inside her high rubber boots. Her feet were cold. A trickle of rain, caught in her collar, crept down the back of her neck, and she shivered.

Part of her wanted to turn back, but she couldn't go home. Joanne would be there, sneering at her. "Where have you been?" she'd say. "You look like a drowned rat." And Momma wouldn't be home till after dark—Momma.

To the west it was clearing, a low sun breaking through the clouds. North, across the meadow, a single car sped toward town. Her fingers were numb. She shoved them into the pockets of her jacket and stepped out into the open.

Their mother had been lucky to get the job in town at the bakery when her husband left. "Eileen," her brothers told her, "he ain't comin' back, you know that. He always was a no-count. Everybody knows where he's gone, him an' that floozie . . ."

"Hush," Gram had said then. "You boys don't know nothin' about it, so just hush up. Leenie, that'll be a good job for you. You always were good in the kitchen."

Eileen's younger brother, Jimmy, moved in that summer.

"Time he got outa the house," Gram said. "He's a big boy now. An' you should have a man around, Leenie. It ain't safe, you bein' alone there, just you an' the girls. What would you do if some stranger showed up?"

Eileen laughed. "I don't know, Ma. Send him on over to you, I guess. You'd know what to do."

"Now Eileen, don't joke with me. You get Jimmy to help you with the chores, you hear? He's strong and willing, but he has to be told. He's drinking too much, an' it'll lead to no end of trouble if you don't keep after him about it."

"But Ma, what am I supposed to do?" Eileen lifted her hands to indicate her helplessness, and Jimmy, who was standing right there, started laughing.

"Jimmy Lee, I'm warning you," Gram sputtered. "You're tempting the Devil!"

Eileen put her hand over her mouth and giggled. "Oh Ma," she said. "The Devil?"

Uncle Jimmy was a profligate, Gram used to say. That's what she called him. Still he filled the house with noisy conversation and unpredictable excitement. He helped with dinner and burned the mashed potatoes. The pot sat filled with water in the sink for three days before it could be scraped clean. Once he nearly burned down the house when he fell asleep smoking a cigarette. It smoldered through the mattress and into the box springs before Eileen woke up. "Jimmy! Jimmy!" she shouted into the smoky room. Beside the bed she found a bottle of beer which she poured into the hole in the mattress after she jerked her brother out of bed. "Aw Sis," he said, when she scolded him. "It was an accident."

"You could have killed us all," she railed, but in fact she was so grateful they had all been spared she soon forgave him. "Gram says your Uncle Jimmy is going to the Devil if he doesn't mend his ways," she told the girls. And they understood, because the Devil was in Hell and Hell was a fiery place, which most certainly suited Uncle Jimmy's present leanings.

Uncle Jimmy protected them from their antagonisms. No one could stay mad at Uncle Jimmy, and he had a way of putting himself in the middle of any fight that started between them.

"Have a beer," he'd say, popping the cap, "it'll cool you off." And Eileen would stop mid-step in an advance on Joanne. She'd push her hair back off her forehead, take the beer out of Uncle Jimmy's hand, and sigh. "You girls are going to drive me crazy," she'd say.

Uncle Jimmy did have a reputation with the bottle. More than once that summer he slept in his car on the side of the road because he was too drunk to drive. "Wait till winter," Eileen said, "he'll freeze to death if he does it then."

It was late August, long before the first frost when the accident happened. Jimmy had been on his way home sometime after midnight when he drove straight into a power pole on the outside curve of the road. The windshield popped out, exploding shards that spat upon the pavement. Jimmy would have sailed out too, but he was pinned from the waist down in crushed metal and securely impaled through the heart by the steering column.

After that, Marla began to put her things in order, to put the house in order—the magazines on the living room table stacked just so. If anyone moved them she straightened them again. She ordered her school books and papers first. Her pencils must all go in the narrow little box in the right hand drawer of the desk. No one must open that drawer, because nothing must be disturbed. Nothing must be disordered. Out of order—the very phrase seemed menacing.

At night she lay in bed and thought about where everything was. She thought about her socks, carefully mated, each pair rolled together at the cuffs and placed in a stack on the left side of the second dresser drawer. She thought about her two blouses hung in the closet with her three dresses and her plaid skirt, her shoes, side by side beneath them. She thought about her brush and comb set neatly on the dresser, and she thought about her school books stacked atop each other according to size, the biggest on the bottom. Uncle Jimmy—why had he abandoned them? Now there was no protection, no safety, nothing to count on. The house seemed bigger without him filling it, and darker and colder. Something was pressing at the edges of things—just outside the black glass of the night windows, in the corners of the closet. Something was pressing in on her. When she closed her eyes, Marla could almost feel it, a hot breath close to her face, eyes glowing like red glass in the dark, sharp teeth. It pressed on her during the day, too, and she had to fight it off. She had to make things tidy, keep things straight, everything where it belonged. Otherwise, whatever it was that pressed in on her would come in completely. And she had to keep it out. And she had to do it alone. There was no one to help her, no way to explain.

In the kitchen, she stacked the pots and pans, the plates and cups and saucers. Joanne made a brief foray into a similar tidyness, but had apparently abandoned it and surrendered to the household chaos, choosing as her point of resistance and control the constant fertile battleground of defiance against their mother. "She loves me!" Joanne had asserted. Yet without Uncle Jimmy, she and her mother fought constantly. And Marla knew it was true, her mother loved Joanne more.

Marla tried not to think about the kitchen when she lay in bed at night, staring into the dark. She tried not to think of the kitchen, and she tried not to think of the toilet that might not flush, and she tried not to think of the shower. She saw spiders there, saw them climb out, growing larger, the red spot on the little black bulb of their bodies growing larger and brighter as they crept toward the bed. She did not like to think of the shower once the lights were off. And as time went by, she found it increasingly difficult to think of the shower at all without imagining the spiders. She had to take the flashlight and search the corners carefully each time, before she turned the water on.

Marla trudged along the edge of the asphalt. The brief sun had sunk behind a stand of maples and the retreating November light was dimmed still further by the low clouds. An occasional crack of thunder rolled over her, and several times she saw lightening branch magically above the horizon. The only other sounds she heard were the squish of her boots in the wet grass and her own breath. Up ahead the forest closed in again and the road led into darkness. She would have to get through the woods before she got to town. Lightening licked the sky to the south and as it disappeared she heard thunder. It faded, save for a distant droning roar. She cocked her head and stood still, listening. The sound came, not from the sky, but from a car heading toward her at the far end of the meadow—a car headed toward town.

Mrs. Sutter pulled over when she saw Marla, and, leaning toward the door, gestured to Marla to get in. Marla hesitated. She did not want to explain to Mrs. Sutter about Joanne. Mrs. Sutter gestured again, impatiently, and then, leaning a little farther, opened the door of the big blue Buick. Marla took a step toward the car, caught the door, and smiled uncertainly.

"For heaven's sake, child, what are you doing out here? It's almost dark. How did you get here?"

"I walked,"

"But where are you going?"

"To town." Marla turned her head slightly to avoid meeting Mrs. Sutter's eyes.

Mrs. Sutter puffed her cheeks between the fluffy fur of her collar. "Well, get in," she commanded. "I'm going to town. Hurry up now, it's cold out. Get in the car."

Mrs. Sutter reminded Marla of Gram. She was big like Gram. But not as old. She had a little boy two grades behind Marla in school. Marla got in the car. She slid in over the smooth seat, feeling her wet dress cold against her bare thighs and the backs of her knees.

"You're not dressed warm enough," Mrs. Sutter remarked as Marla tugged the heavy door closed. "Are you all right, Marla? There's no trouble, is there?" she asked as she pulled back onto the road.

Marla stared straight ahead at the asphalt. It was new. They had redone the road last summer. She remembered the smell of it and the big roller they had driven over it to make it smooth. "No," she said.

It grew suddenly darker as they drove into the woods.

"I'll take you to the bakery," Mrs. Sutter said. "Your mother's there, isn't she?"

"Yes." Marla had her hand on the seat beside her. Her fingers brushed against the pair of gloves that lay there next to Mrs. Sutter's purse. She stole a glance at them. How like her mother's they were, the same dark leather, smooth and soft. Exactly like her mother's except for the rabbit fur lining. Mrs. Sutter's gloves were lined with something else, fleece maybe. Marla gazed down at the gloves and fingered the edge where the leather and lining met. Yes, fleece.

"Those are my gloves."

Marla turned, surprised. She stared at the gloves in her hand. Stricken, she tried to explain. "I know," she began, "it's just. . . . They're very nice." She tried to say the right thing. She wanted Mrs. Sutter to understand. "They're like my mother's," she said finally.

"Well, they're not your mother's." Mrs. Sutter was firm, and Marla hung her head in confusion and shame.

"I'm sorry," she said, although she did not know exactly what she should be sorry about.

The lights of the bakery shone bright and friendly through the windows, though the glass was too fogged up to be able to see more than the movement of shapes inside. Mrs. Sutter stopped the car. "Here we are," she said.

Marla eased herself toward the door. She was out of the car now and anxious to be left alone.

"You go in to your mother, before you catch a chill."

"Yes, ma'am. Thank you for the ride." Marla closed the door and turned away. She heard Mrs. Sutter's car pull out into the street and drive off as she walked up the sidewalk toward the bakery.

Inside it was warm and steamy and smelled of fresh bread. Her mother had on the big white apron she wore at work. "Marla," she said, surprised and puzzled when her daughter came in. She smelled of flour when she held Marla in her arms. She dried Marla's hair on one of the big white linen cloths that weren't really for anything like drying hair, but were for covering the breads and rolls while they were rising. "This will do," her mother had said. They drove home together, the car smelling of bread from the fresh loaf they brought with them.

Rain beat against the windshield. It was pitch dark and silent, except for the engine and the wipers' rhythmic swish-swish, swish-swish. Marla wanted to sit closer to her mother, but she wasn't sure it would be all right. Once they were out of town, she felt her mother drifting. When lightning lit the interior of the car, she glanced at her mother's face and saw, as she expected, Eileen's gaze fixed on the road with the familiar vacant look Marla knew so well. And she knew that her mother's thoughts were far away. Only Joanne could keep their mother in the present. The way they fought was terrifying, but it made them real. It kept them there. Marla wished for a moment that she were Joanne. Joanne was willing to risk everything in the battle. She acted with no thought of consequences, said whatever came into her head and attacked like an animal, with snarls and fists and clawing nails. Eileen and Joanne were alike in that way, and Marla was different—too timid to stand up for herself, and frightened of the physical violence that had become an almost daily routine between her mother and Joanne, now that the three were alone in the house.

Eileen had begun to hum softly as they drove along, and then she said, in a dreamy voice, "The sun is probably shining in California."

Marla considered this statement. She thought that the sun was probably not shining in California because it was night now. She knew that when it was night, the sun was on the other side of the world. And California wasn't exactly the other side of the world. China was more like the other side of the world, or Africa.

Her mother continued. "I think California would be nice now, all that sun, and the ocean. I'd like to see the ocean."

She fell silent again, and Marla's skin began to prickle. She knew her mother was thinking. She was thinking about California, about seeing the ocean, about being far away from where she was right this minute.

"Momma," Marla began, and then stopped.

"I'd like to go to California," Eileen said.

Marla's heart sank. Eileen began to hum again, and Marla sat very still beside her, waiting, a kind of hopeless waiting, as if for a blow to be struck, as if for some pain that would mark the end of the helplessness and tension she felt.

Eileen stopped humming and was quiet. After a while she spoke again. "Maybe we'll go to California," she said, "you and me and Joanne."

Marla relaxed. She began to breathe once again and wriggled her feet in little up and down swings, tapping the heels of her rubber boots against the bottom front of the car seat.

Eileen broke into song. "California here I come, right back where I started from," she trilled, and then interrupted herself. "Your Uncle Jimmy was in California. Said there were more oranges on one tree than a person could eat in a whole winter. And rows and rows of those trees."

"Where's Momma? When is she coming home?"

"Hush now," Gram said. "You're coming with me and Uncle Gary. Do you have everything?"

"But we want Momma. Where is she?"

Gram pulled her hankie out of her pocket and wiped her eyes. "You girls listen to me now. Your momma's gone away for a while. We're going to my house, you and me and Uncle Gary."

"When is she coming home?" They tugged at Gram's arms and begged her to tell when, oh when, would their mother come home?

Marla's hand was in the coat pocket, her fingers curled into the soft dark leather. She thought suddenly of holding hands. It was like holding hands with someone's spirit because the hand itself was not there. But she could imagine it. She imagined it all right. How many times had she opened the drawer of her mother's dresser, quietly, and looked down on the pair of black leather gloves that always lay there, just inside, just on top. And she had stroked them. And closed the drawer carefully, sliding the smooth wood over wood, back into place.

In the semi-darkness of the bedroom now, bent over the pile of coats, she drew her hand slowly out of the pocket. Through the door and down the hall she heard the sounds of conversation. Slowly she drew her hand away from the pocket, and with it the pair of gloves. *Those are my gloves.* And then—someone in the hall, the door opening.

"Why Marla, here you are. We were just starting to wonder."

Marla turned quickly, too quickly, dropping the gloves into the pile of coats. "I was just," she stammered. "I was just looking for my coat."

"Are you leaving? Already?"

"No, I . . . I had my comb in the pocket." She paused.

"Here, use mine."

Marla reached. It seemed a long way. It seemed a long time. And then the comb was in her hand. She stood in front of the mirror, lifting the comb to her hair. "I am Marla," she thought to herself, "daughter of Eileen. My mother's daughter. My mother did love me. She always loved me."

❦

WHILE THE DISTANCE WIDENS

WHILE THE DISTANCE WIDENS

"THEY HAVE A GIRL working there," Elaine told me one day. I was more interested in the baked chicken we were eating. "Did you talk to her?"

"I don't think you could call it a conversation. She seems shy. I thought she was a kid at first—a man, I mean, just young. But then I saw her hair was in a pony tail." Elaine laughed, pleased at her recollection. "She has the most wonderful grey-green eyes."

I suppose it caught my imagination—the thought of a young woman adjusting the valves of my wife's car. What would such a creature be like? But the conversation moved on, and as I thought about the expense of new brakes, I forgot about the image of a girl grease monkey. Till one Monday morning when I went to the bird sanctuary out on the coast.

I go there to write. Well, more to mull things over, although occasionally I jot notes. That morning my mind was full of an argument I had begun to hear and was still trying to place: a man and woman, not a couple, perhaps mother and son or brother and sister. The bleachers were empty, as usual, except for a lone figure that turned out to be Sara. She was hunched under a thick wool sweater with a turtleneck collar that covered the ends of her hair. I couldn't tell from the distance whether she was male or female. It's hard, in any case, to think of Sara as a woman. She seems more a perennial adolescent—her face with its grey eyes, thin nose and chapped lips, bare of make-up, hardly more than a child's. On the other hand, the older I get, the younger young people seem to be, so I can no longer trust my first impressions.

Close up I saw that Sara's hair was streaked dishwater blond against the light brown underhair, like the undercoats of certain setters, the dogs my father kept for hunting. I remember one in particular, a high-strung in-bred retriever named Lacy, whose delicate fine-boned legs had a perpetual tremor, so she appeared to shiver as if she were constantly cold.

Sara was munching potato chips. Half a tuna sandwich and the crust of the other half lay on the bench beside her, on top of a wax paper bag.

"Hi," I said. "Can you see anything?" She looked up at me, licking her fingers and squinting into the fog.

"Nope," she pronounced, after licking her thumb. She folded the empty chip bag carefully in half and half again, flattening the shiny paper. When she finished, she looked back at me as if surprised I was still there.

"Mind if I sit down?"

She glanced around, taking in the empty bleachers. "Suit yourself." She moved to gather up the sandwich, hesitated, and held it toward me. "Want half a tuna sandwich?"

I wasn't really hungry, but I read once that it's a terrible rejection, not to mention an insult in tribal cultures, to refuse a gift, especially food; so I make it a practice always to accept such offerings. I took the sandwich from her outstretched hand and sat down.

"Do you come here often?" She didn't answer. Instead she moved ever so slightly, contracting away from me.

"You remind me of someone," I said, sure that she did, but unable to place who it was. Something crossed her eyes then, like a shadow, and though her face remained impassive, it seemed to stiffen. She was looking me square in the eyes when she spoke again.

"Are you a pervert?"

I was shocked. "No. Of course not. This is a bird sanctuary. I'm a bird watcher." I wanted to laugh, but I realized then that she was really frightened. "I'm a married man," I said, as if that were evidence of my harmlessness, and I held my left hand out to show her my ring.

"So," she said, recoiling from my hand.

"I mean . . ." What did I mean? She stood up. I stood up. "Don't go. I'll go. I'm sorry, I didn't mean to . . ." She had started to walk away. I followed her. "I didn't mean to frighten you. This is terrible. Please stop." No one had ever been afraid of me before, not even my own children. What had I done? Did I look like a dirty old man? "Please!" I begged her.

She turned around. "I am not afraid of you," she said carefully, but she was trembling. I sat down. What a dunderhead! How could I act like such a jerk? Was I acting like a jerk? Like a pervert? When I looked up, it was my turn to be surprised. She was still there.

"I guess you're not,"

"Not what?"

"A pervert."

"Oh, that. No," I said sadly, "not a pervert. A blunderer maybe, but not a pervert." I still had her sandwich in my hand. "But don't you know you can't offer food to old strays? They start wagging their tails and getting all friendly."

"Is that what you were doing?"

"What was I supposed to do? Take your sandwich and leave?"

"Why not?"

"I don't know." I was suddenly weary.

"After all," she continued, musing to herself as much as to me, puzzled by me, as if I were a stray dog, "you did come up here to the top bench right where I was sitting. You could have sat anywhere. We're the only ones here. It's not like there's no place else to sit."

"But this is where I always sit. It's the best place to see their nests from."

"Do you come here often?" she mimicked.

I could see she wasn't afraid anymore. "What were you going to do," I asked, "call the police?"

Her eyes got bigger, and then she giggled. "Anyway," she said, "I do come here. Every so often. But what a line! And who, pray tell, do I remind you of?"

"You don't have to rub my nose in it. You do remind me of someone."

"Do I really?" Mocking me again, I could see it in her eyes.

"Yes, but I can't think who." My god, could it be my daughter, Susan?

*   *   *

Sara and Susan do look a little alike, but in hindsight, I think that Sara reminded me of myself, the same way Susan reminds me of myself with her odd reticence and her pretense of self-confidence.

"I did think you were a pervert," Sara told me later.

"Why didn't you run?"

"Run? My legs were shaking so bad I wasn't sure I could walk."

"And I thought you were making a dignified exit. Were you really afraid of me?"

"Really."

"But you didn't run."

"I thought it would be safer to pretend I wasn't afraid. My mother told me this story once about being grabbed by a guy in Central Park. He just leaped out of the bushes and picked her up and started to run with her slung over his shoulder."

I tried to imagine this. The man in my mind was more simian than human, not quite King Kong, but close. I envisioned his arms extra long, his torso bent forward drastically from the waist. I saw the woman over his shoulder wearing a skirt, stockings and high heels, a Lois Lane type, I thought, getting the stories mixed up. "What did she do?"

"That's the point. She had this strategy. She decided not to do anything, just go limp. She didn't even scream."

"What happened?"

"Eventually he got tired, I guess. And he just dropped her and ran off. She said he wanted her to fight, and when she didn't, he lost interest. Her idea was that the fuss was part of what guys like that are turned on by. Anyway, that's what I got out of the story."

"Do you believe that?"

Sara comtemplated me with those wary grey eyes of hers and chewed her lip. After a while she said, "I don't know. I guess I never really decided. I used to think, probably because of that story—and maybe some other things she must have said—that it was safer not to resist. But actually I think it would be better to fight back. If I got picked up and slung over some guy's shoulder, I think I'd kick and scratch and yell bloody murder."

"And run if you could?"

"Yes, certainly."

"But you didn't run from me."

"You hadn't really done anything yet. So I thought if I pretended to be calm I could bluff you. I guess my mother's story sank in that much. You know, act like you're cool and the world will be too intimidated to encroach."

"You do it all the time, Sara."

"What?"

"Pretend." She had that wary look in her eyes again.

"I think you're full of shit," she said.

I shrugged. "So?" That was her line.

*   *   *

I haven't told you about Elaine. Funny, I'm not sure Sara even knows her name. Elaine and I have been married sixteen years. We know so little when we fall in love — so little about how things accumulate between people, how the web of events thickens and grows more dense. You hardly feel it happening. It's a strange snare, living with someone, making a family. One day you realize you're caught, like it or not. You're entangled, too entangled to ever separate.

Elaine has an inviolate sense of privacy. And from that — I think from that — a deep inner peace, a pool of quiet I cannot fathom. And what her quiet touches, it seems to smooth and soften. I watch her fold the laundry, or close her eyes for a moment at the piano, and see a smile drift across her face. Does she hear music? Oh, yes. She hears the music of heaven in the most mundane of sounds: the whir of the spin cycle, the drip of the faucet, children's voices from the yard, a dog barking down the street, the clicking of my computer, the refrigerator door opening, and even her own voice, "Close the refrigerator," which is something she must say thirty times a day. (Do all children hang on the refrigerator door, staring into the cold shelves, forgetting, if ever they knew, what is was they wanted?) "Close the refrigerator," a clear calm voice, patient to the last.

Elaine moves toward patches of light, dreaming into the sun while she works, stopping periodically to listen, her listening like a meditation, a gathering from source, from light itself. Whatever it is she needs, Elaine takes it from the sun. And from the random sounds of life around her, and she is sustained. And she sustains us, her family. She puts sounds together. These are compositions. The titles are always unadorned. "Living Room," she called one piece the New Ensemble performed last fall. Piano, reeds, and percussion. Reality is enough for Elaine. She doesn't need embellishment. She doesn't need drama. "Life is dramatic all by itself," she says, "don't you think?" And she smiles her paradoxically enigmatic and utterly open smile, laughter in her eyes. I wonder sometimes if Elaine is laughing at me, if there is something she knows that I don't, some joke I am missing. I trust her. And yet, I don't always know myself, and sometimes I feel foolish in my ignorance.

*   *   *

Sara was the only woman mechanic in the dealer's shop. When Eddie was hired to do body work in the next complex, he could barely believe his eyes. At first he thought she was a long hair—some scrawny punk kid, he told her later. But once he discovered she was a girl, he found himself wondering about her.

She often ate lunch at the cafe down the block. Eddie had seen her there, sitting alone at a table by the window, reading a book or staring out while she ate French fries and sipped a milkshake. Without her coveralls, she was a slight person, too slight to be even a small man, though she might have passed for a boy. He watched her from the corner of his eye, her profile lit by the window. Eventually he asked if he could eat with her.

I picture him approaching the table. She is unaware of him until he speaks and startles her. "Mind if I join you?" he asks. If this scene sounds familiar, it is because I imagine it rather like my own first words with Sara, which came later, and seemed in some way a repetition of their meeting.

There is something about Sara—her apparent preoccupation, her peculiar distance or shyness—whatever it is, one often has the feeling of intruding upon her, at least I have, and I imagine Eddie did, too. When I think of this, I empathize with Eddie, who as it turns out, is far less articulate than I, and even more vulnerable than Sara. Of all of us, oddly enough, it is Eddie toward whom I feel the strongest sympathy.

About their courtship I know little. Sara's stories were really about the time they lived together, the time during which I met her. I tried to listen between the lines to what she told me, to understand what she felt for Eddie. I decided finally that it had to do with a longing to heal him. I think it was her own loneliness she saw in him. Her dreams were filled with wounded men, rough violent men, whose eyes were dark with anger and loneliness. She knew what they wanted, she told me. They wanted her to love them, and she felt she ought to.

Sara was not wise. She did not know how to be careful anymore than she knew how to be glamorous, anymore than she knew how to shade her eye makeup just so, the way the magazine said: shiny silver on the center of the lid, blended into midnight blue for evening or pale fawn for the office. She slams the current issue of *Mademoiselle* back into the stand with irritation and reaches for a copy of *Popular Mechanics*. But she can't concentrate, replaces the magazine and turns to walk down the aisle.

Eddie is standing near the end of the stacks. She almost bumps into him when she rounds the corner. He holds a large hardbound book, *Antarctica* emblazoned in gold letters on the blue cover.

"Oh! What are you doing here?"

"I was waiting for you."

"You were?" She doesn't ask why. Sara never pursues personal questions when she is startled. She looks at the book instead. "What are you reading?"

"Penguins. There are seventeen different kinds of them."

"I know." She isn't really listening. She is thinking about the way he looked before he saw her—the angle of his head, the back of his neck, the soft hair that curls around his ears. Even now, as he stands before her, she remains disarmed by the lost boy she saw beneath the man.

No, Sara was not wise, and what she saw, or imagined she saw beneath the surface of the world, hurt her. So she withdrew from it, from the world of people, and pulled into herself, into birds, and into her world of repairs. She could not fix people, but she could fix things.

She could not fix Eddie, but she knew how to fix his brakes. She could not rebuild a battered heart, her own or the world's, but she could rebuild a carburetor. She thought about it that way, though she couldn't quite say so. "You know," she told me once, "the carburetor is the heart of the car."

*   *   *

Women disturbed Eddie, fancy women with red lips and eyes lined like a mink's, women with red nails and dangling earrings and clinking bracelets. He could see the hunger in their bodies pressed into tight pants and leaning toward him over the counter in the shop. He saw the eager nervousness in their shining mouths and quick pink tongues. He saw the predatory arching of their fingers, the nails gleaming, and he saw through this, underneath this, their panic. It was their panic that disturbed him most of all. It was their panic he wanted to escape, the panic packed into their taut bodies, precariously placed atop their high-heeled shoes.

The goldfish fins itself around to face him, its eyes staring fixedly through the glass, then turns again and flicks into the corner of the aquarium. Eddie stares after it, his mind on the white expanse of the farthest place he can imagine, Antarctica. Maybe it isn't the penguins. His eyes jerk back to the woman before him. He stands quietly, like a well-trained horse being saddled. He shifts his weight from one foot to the other, while she holds him with her conversation, with her spike-heeled words. He blinks, his eyes slipping slightly out of focus for a moment, blurring the red mouth, a bright smear across the wavering shape of her face, the smear kaleidoscopically shifting with the sounds he knows are words. And then, he pulls himself back, blinking again, nods, answers the question, all the while waiting to be released.

Eddie returns from his daydreams as he returns from sleep to waking, confident of his body; he pours himself into it like liquid into a carton, body as container. It moves at his wish, easily, readily, without objection. Only occasionally, his left shoulder aches from the dislocation he suffered playing baseball when he was in high school. It aches now, as he stands there waiting for the woman with the red mouth to go away. It makes him angry to have to stand there, to be trapped in the mesh of appropriate responses and obligations.

His mother never wears red polish. "Oh, no. Not at my age," she says smiling—not at all the desperate terrifying smile she smiled when he was little. He has almost forgotten. The woman with the red mouth reminds him, but he cannot exactly remember. "I'm not as young as I used to be," his mother says. "Anyway, it just chips. I don't have time for it."

A woman her age. What is her age? She refuses to tell even the police. "It's none of their business how old I am. It's not nice to ask a lady her age, if she's young or old. I know my rights. And I know when they're out of line. I wasn't born yesterday, that's what I tell them."

Eddie eyes her cautiously. He doesn't really remember the red nails, but he remembers the look in her eyes, the set of her lips and the tone of her voice, which seems now to be inside his own head, wheedling and cajoling him: "Eddie. . . ." her firm grip on his arm, and those nails, those nails digging into his skin.

The red mouth reminds him of something. The voice is familiar, not the words, but the sound of the voice, honey over the edge of fear. He takes a step back. "I'll bring your car around," he says.

He isn't really interested in penguins so much as he likes the pictures, because there are no people in them. All that white expanse of ice is comforting. He'd like to go there. He'd like to go to the desert, too—drive or walk, he wouldn't mind walking those miles and miles of emptiness, just dunes and tiny occasional plants, not even animal tracks, because of the wind and certainly no human footprints. But in his dream, he is near the ocean. He groans in his sleep. Above him, bats circle in a clear twilight sky, and below the cliff, the water rises steadily, while he looks the other way. Then it is noon and a white light flattens the shapes of things, diminishing him and what happens around him. He feels suddenly that he can't breathe. The oxygen has been sucked from the sky and the atmosphere collapses like an empty balloon. His brothers have disappeared down a trail beside the cliff. On the path in front of him an enormous snake slides from the grass blocking his way. It stares at him with sulky eyes and flicks its tongue in a lazy warning: you can go no further until you deal with me.

He opens his eyes with a start and feels in the dark that Sara is awake, too. He could pull her to him then or roll toward her. He could cross the line between them. Doesn't he want that? Isn't she waiting for him?

*   *   *

I don't know what to make of this world. The older I get, the stranger it seems. The way we keep making the same stupid mistakes over and over, generation after generation. I don't know what I'm supposed to think when the gas station attendant wears a sleeveless black tee shirt with big white lettering FIGHT CRIME, and right below it in small script, running off the right side of his chest it says: shoot back. I ponder this as I poke the nozzle of unleaded premium into the mouth of my gas tank. Is it supposed to be funny? Another joke I don't get? Or is this an announcement of the man's stance in life. Shoot back. One way to operate, I guess.

I think of the elderly woman I read about in the newspaper who crouched and fired, plugging the burglar just above the heart. A drug crazed criminal with a long record, he had shot at her first, ripping a hole in the shoulder pad of her coat. He died, but not before he managed to run, spouting a trail of blood, all the way back to his house nearly a mile away. I sympathized with the old lady. She was obviously protecting her interests, her life at that point. Something out of the wild west. The pump clicks off under my palm. A full tank. I pay the attendant and get back in my car.

Pulling out of the station I turn the radio on to hear the closing strains of "Only You," a tune I remember well. Close-dancing in a darkened room. The scent of eau de toilette on the warm skin of sixteen-year-old. Not a song Sara and Eddie would remember. If I were home, I would take Elaine in my arms and slow-dance her across the living room. I would place my hand at the small of her back and pull her close, press my thigh against her, my lips to her ear. I can almost hear her laugh, low and soft.

* * *

At home, Elaine sits by the window in a moment alone. Susan is at school, Luke at day care, and a quiet fills the house, a temporary lull in the afternoon. A warm sun, filtered by the bamboo shade, lays slits of light across her lap. A small breeze slaps the shade intermittently against the wall. The cat leaps down from the sill, paw bumping the brass bowl set there so it raps once and settles into place again: rap-tap-tap. Blocks away a car backfires. The cat pads softly across the hardwood floor, disappears into the kitchen. Some small bird calls cheerily from the locust trees, twi twi twi, twi twi twi, then stops. Slap, slap, the bamboo blind continues, and the leaves whisper. Elaine lifts her cup, drinks, sets it back down (tink, cup against saucer), then moves from the window toward the piano. She will remember each sound.

In the old house, the grand piano gleamed a glossy black like a great beast in the living room. Divided pane windows lined up across the south wall. Beneath them, Elaine curled on the cushions of the window seat to sit in the sun or watch raindrops crawl down the glass, bump over the wood cross piece, and continue down the next pane.

The house sat on the edge of town, half-way up a round hill, in front of a wood, an old rambling house that Elaine's mother could not keep up with, a house in some disrepair, the sills in need of paint, the yard overgrown. Inside, things were a constant lively disorder. It was a house that was hard to leave; there were a thousand little things to attend to just at the moment of departure: windows to close, doors to lock, animals to be put out or in.

And it was a house that was easy to come home to, easy to open the heavy front door, slide out of boots in the entry way, set books or packages down on the nearest table, and find oneself in the midst of the friendly chaos of home—voices and laughter, cats under foot, a pet turtle ambling across the oriental carpet, a vase of drooping roses, a coffee table littered with crayons, magazines, seashells, and photographs, someone always arriving or departing. It was a house that was big enough to have quiet corners, and Elaine was often in a quiet corner: on the window seat with her drawing pens and paper, or at the bench of the black piano, her small hands moving experimentally over the keys, slowly picking out the notes that seemed to fit into the other sounds of the house, for Elaine was always listening to a larger sound than what she played, listening to all the sounds in her house and playing a harmony, a discord, a melody, in relation to them.

On the piano was a photograph. In the picture, two men with a woman between them walk down a city street arm in arm. The woman's calves are thin, and the line of her shin bone is visible down the front of one leg as she steps forward. Her shoes look heavy at the end of those slender legs and narrow ankles. The men on either side are her brothers. The youngest wears a uniform, the other wears a suit and tie, and although he is older, he is nearer the woman's height, shorter than his younger brother. Together they stride toward the camera with a cheerful confidence that belies the future.

Elaine never thought to wonder until years later who had taken the picture. Perhaps it was her father. She had not thought of him in connection with the picture, partly because it seemed the trio was completely self-contained, an impenetrable unit that long preceeded her father's arrival. Still later it occurred to Elaine that of course her father had been there. Perhaps his presence had only been unimaginable because the photograph preceeded her own arrival, and it seemed impossible that her father could have existed prior to her own existence.

This photograph stood in a gold gilt frame atop the grand piano in the old house, and when her mother died Elaine took the photograph to her own house, along with the piano, which no one beside her mother and she had ever really played. So the photograph and the piano remained together, and Elaine looked often in their faces, into the merry eyes of her youngest uncle, who had died overseas not long after she was born, her mother who had kept that uncle alive with stories, and her second uncle, the last living member of her mother's family. She plays for them, her strange, sometimes tuneless pieces that catch the memories of the old house and weave them together with the sounds of her life now: her children's voices, her husband's rumbling laughter, and the outside world with its weather, its endless cycles that enclose them all.

Her husband's rumbling laughter. My laughter, for it is of myself I write as I listen, not in the way my wife does as a composer of music, but as a man listens in constant wonder to the familiar sounds of his own house. I listen and I write, puzzling over our lives, how we fit together, all of us. Puzzling over how to hold this precious web that continues to grow, that has caught us, Elaine and me and the kids, and yet invites others. I listen, attentive to see how they belong, anxious not to make a rent in the delicate weaving of our lives.

*   *   *

Sara chews the inside of her mouth as well as her nails when she is anxious. She is a muncher. She munches apples while she talks on the phone, staring at her reflection in the hall window as if it were someone else, a stranger.

"Are you all right?" her mother asks. "Sara, have you got a cold?"

"No."

"You sound muffled. Maybe it's a bad connection."

"You're loud and clear."

"Sara, are you eating something?"

"Uh huh."

She munches celery while she thumbs through the latest issue of *Technology Illustrated.* Celery with peanut butter.

"Hi, peanut breath," Eddie greets her.

"Hi yourself," she grins, giving him a quick kiss.

Potato chips, corn chips, popcorn—salted. It seems to Eddie that she is always licking salt off her fingers, carefully and slowly, the way a cat cleans its paws, while she thinks of something else. He never knows what she is thinking. And it never occurs to her to tell him.

*   *   *

Eddie has told Sara that it drives him crazy the way she eats. And she has told me this. I try to imagine what he means. I imagine them at the dinner table. Does he wolf his food like a GI in the mess hall? He seems a man detached from his senses, a man who does not notice the roses she places on his bureau, does not notice the daisies she has put in the yellow vase on the table where they are eating. Let us imagine he has served the food. His own plate is piled high with spaghetti. Thick tomato sauce flows over the mound of soft pasta. Sara is in awe of his appetite.

She watches him twirl his fork in the mixture of ground meat and red sauce. Her own plate, she notices, looks twice as big because there is less on it. The pale blue pottery edges out from the little volcano of food, and looking down she can't help feeling slightly rejected. Rejected? Did she tell me that. Not exactly, but that is what I heard between the lines. Because her serving seems so stingy compared with his. Why should she feel denied, like a poor relative?

The heartiness of Eddie's appetite makes her feel small and somehow ashamed of her own puny hunger. She should be hungrier! She should be able to eat more. I can eat more than he can, she thinks, just not all at once. I probably do eat more! She thinks this with a secret sense of victory. Little does he know. But she can't help feeling she should be offered more, encouraged to eat more. If he cared for her he would coax her. He would put more food on her plate, and he would urge her to eat, not just sit there shoveling food in his mouth like there was no tomorrow. She pushes her pasta with her fork, nudging it under the blanket of sauce. Now she isn't hungry at all. She can't eat. Eddie has half-demolished his plateful and she is only fussing with her third bite.

Sara's mother always cooks too much food. The fullness of the refrigerator used to upset Sara. She felt she was supposed to keep up with the endless flow of food. She was overwhelmed by that refrigerator, and by her mother's constant admonitions that she should eat more, or how would she grow up to be big and strong? Her brothers were big and strong. They had appetites. They didn't pick at their food. They ate their food like human beings. She eats like a bird, and she looks like a bird, too, her brothers say, with her skinny stick arms and legs and her pointed little face and her fluttering hands. And the way she likes to live at the top of the tree. Does she think that's what she is, a bird?

That refrigerator is a constant reproach, jammed with special treats at all times: fresh berries and cream, leftover chicken, a roast waiting for that evening's oven, potato salad, English muffins, juice, fresh vegetables.

Her father's refrigerator is a different story. Unidentifiable leftovers molding in diminutive containers, lost behind the plastic bag with two kiwi in it. A half dozen eggs (her mother would never think of buying eggs by the *half* dozen), two small cartons of fruit yogurt. Her father's refrigerator feels empty, constricted. He buys butter a cube at a time, the way Sara used to when she was in college, not because she wanted to buy it that way, but because she didn't have the money for a pound.

Would she have bought a pound then, if she had had the money? How long does it take one girl to eat a pound of butter, a girl who doesn't cook all that much? "Come home, Sara. Come home and get a decent meal," her mother would beg. And at home there would be lemon meringue pie, mounds of mashed potatoes with butter pressed into a deep pool. And there would be bacon and scrambled eggs for breakfast, with toast and jam and milk and orange slices, or pancakes drowned in syrup. And Sara would complain, "I can't eat all this, Mother. It's too much." Her brothers would tease her: "Same old sticks. Same old bird."

Eddie has cleaned his plate by now, and Sara feels even more slighted, jealous of his food and his appetite, angry that he is getting up to have seconds. But how can she be angry at him for eating? So she says nothing. They eat in a silence he seems not to notice. She wishes he were interested in her. She wants to tell him about her plans, but she is pulling so far inside she thinks she will never find a way out.

But she has me now. She can tell me about the silence while she and Eddie eat. She can tell me about Eddie's big plate of food and her own sad little helping. And when she does, she ends up laughing.

"Here, I brought you some bird seed." I hand her a bag of peanuts. She loves peanuts! "Don't forget to chew," I tell her. "Don't forget you have teeth, strange bird that you are."

She thinks I know her better than anyone. Better than she knows herself. She munches contentedly as she sits beside me on the bench. I

raise my binoculars and she follows the line of my sight to the tops of
the cypress trees across from us. "There," I say, for the moment satis-
fied. And so is she.

*   *   *

"You don't have to yell, I can hear you." Sara speaks quietly. She
means to sound firm, not angry. Certainly not hurt, but in fact as she
speaks she thinks with surprise, almost shame, that she sounds as if
she might cry. Eddie doesn't answer. Instead he stares out the window,
his mouth tight with impatience. He sighs.

"I only meant," he begins, "what's the point?" That's all. I just
want to know what you're trying to say."

Sara feels the stubbornness in herself stand up like an old
woman, like her grandmother, arms folded across her bosom, her jaw
set. She feels her grandmother inside her, the part of herself that
chooses the power of silence, and she cannot answer him. She will not
let him diminish her by making her explain.

"The point is," she says finally, "that I don't have to try to make
you understand. I'm doing this for myself, not for you." A moment
before she had thought she might cry, now she is frightened.

In her grandmother's house she was the scrawny child with hair
as straight and dry as bleached straw. Sara, the child with skinned
knees and bruised elbows, with thighs scraped and scarred from tree-
climbing in her shorts—not with the boys, her brothers did not let her
play with them, but alone. Alone she climbed the cherry tree to the
very top and looked out over the horizon of the world. From the cherry
tree, she could see the house roof, the attic window where she had
placed her crayon pies the summer before—crimped foil tins still
gleamed from the window sill. And there they were, her brothers, far
out on the other side of the field, near the trees. She imagined herself
suddenly released from the branches, soaring over the roof and the
wall, out over the black earth.

Sara has always wanted to fly, wanted the rush of air against her
face, the weightlessness. She dreams it. It doesn't matter whether she
actually flies, it is enough to imagine. She clings to her memory of

climbing the cherry tree, her recollection of being part of the tree as she held herself to its branches, of being part of the wind as the branches swayed and she with them. Her own small breath moved inside her at the same time she was part of a larger life that had its own breath. The earth and everything on it was a great and singular creature. She floated on that creature's breath, hidden in the foliage of the upper branches, which were thin and bent with her weight. She was not really alone, she was part of the movement of leaves, part of the dark trunk, sunk and rooted, part of all the bright and fading blossoms, the sweet fruit.

"Sara."

She is back in her kitchen. Were they arguing? They might have been. She turns the thought in her mind, watching it drift like a leaf on the surface of a stream. Still she will not speak. She doesn't have words anymore. There is no human language for what she feels. She watches Eddie walk toward her, as if he were quite unrelated to her. He looks into her eyes.

"This is silly, Sara," he says.

She would like to look away. But she knows she musn't. She has to suffer this, or he will not let her be.

"Yes," she answers, "you're right, it's silly." But don't try to stop me, she is thinking, though she could not say from doing what. And she is thinking she won't talk about this again, because she will not let him laugh at her, at her ideas. He is part of the world, and the world is different. The world of people and inside and, yes, that world is alone and lonely. Here in the kitchen, with Eddie's questions and his judgements, she is truly alone.

In this small room, with all its cheerful domesticity—the teapot on the shelf, the yellow walls, the tins of spices—she feels a sudden tightness, as if the door to a trap has just sprung shut. Wildly she thinks: the heart that is beating here beneath these ribs, how I feel it pounding! The heart of the earth that is in all things, even houses and sidewalks, I want that heart to beat stronger and stronger. What disorder might there be if we fed that heart instead of starving it? Freeways buckling, buildings talking to us as we enter and exit, walls cracking open, spilling seeds, sprouting and blooming. And with these thoughts there rose in her such a tension she felt she might suffocate.

* * *

I did not laugh at Sara when she talked about flying. That was why she loved birds, just as I did, because they flew. Watching them, she could imagine herself in the air. It was as if Sara did not want to be human, as if being human were a punishment to her. People confused her. She did not feel that she was one of them. She was a spirit caught between worlds, half in and half out of a body she did not know what to do with. Certainly she had never learned to love it. How could she, it did not have wings?

Sara's silence had a sullenness about it that she didn't see. She didn't realize that her moments of inarticulateness were something she and Eddie shared, that his silence when they fought, when she asked him a question, waited an eternity for him to answer, might be a similar combination of fear and resentment. "Tell me," he says. "What is it?" he asks. And she will not speak.

What would happen if he reached for her, held her tight and whispered to her, "I need you. Talk to me. Tell me." But he is too angry and afraid. "All right, don't talk," he says. "Come here," he could have added. She might turn her head away, not wanting him to see into her. He might say, "Please," and she might come to him, and then everything would be different. But he does not say come, and he does not say please.

What if he had just moved, fast? He could do that. He was lithe and strong, though not a large man. She is standing near the door and takes a step toward it, reaches for the knob. But he catches her wrist before she gets there. "Sara," he might have said, "I won't let you go." She starts to pull away, and he steps closer, placing his body beside hers, not touching her. Still, she won't look at him.

He moves and she moves with him, to maintain the distance between them, still not touching. He doesn't wait now, but leans toward her, his mouth by her ear, breath against her skin. And he leans into her slowly, until he is pressed against her. "Let's not talk anymore," he says. "I'm so tired of trying to talk."

For a moment she might have felt trapped. For a moment her heart would have hammered against her ribs so he felt it like the heart of a small animal, frightened and fragile. And then she might have quieted. The sheer pressure of his presence, solid enough to contain her fear, solid enough to calm her, might have changed everything. Imagine her relaxing, beginning to sense her own body, that alien self she wants so often to escape. He could have helped her to inhabit it. He could have done this, or something like this. I have not imagined it perfectly. But I believe Eddie could have broken through, and it would have made all the difference. Why didn't he? That is what puzzles me now. Why did he let the distance widen and widen again?

* * *

"Why do you come here? Why do you talk to me? What do you want?" Sara scrunched her eyes up as she asked me these questions. It was the first thing she said to me that morning after she arrived in a black humor and plopped herself down beside me on the bench without a word.

I answered her slowly. "I would say I didn't want anything. But I don't trust that answer. I don't know why I come, except that I've done it for years." I was hedging, avoiding the real questions. "It's different now that you come, too," I admitted. "Look Sara, if I knew the answers to those questions maybe I wouldn't come anymore."

"What?"

I was beginning to feel uneasy, as if the wariness I saw in Sara had settled in me. "I write because I want to understand," I said, hoping this would satisfy her, but she was after something else.

"What? What do you want to understand?"

"Everything." I paused. "You."

"Why me?"

She wanted to know how I felt about her, wanted me to say it. It was exactly what I had been afraid to ask myself. "I can't answer that," I said. "If I answer it will change something." If I said what came first it would be dangerous for both of us.

Sara sighed, then took a deep breath. "Well," she said, "let me tell you about this week," and she laughed. "You'll love this chapter. It was raining again. You know how it's been. I was bringing up the wood. I had to side-step a pile of feathers on the bottom step, something the cat got, I guess. I stacked the logs and got the fire going. After that I went into the bathroom and combed my hair, which was sticking out in all directions and much too short."

Sara had cut her long hair off, in some sort of fit apparently, the week before. I still hadn't gotten used to it, though in a way it suited her. It had the effect, which she couldn't see, of emphasizing her delicate features. She continued her story.

"I washed my face and marched out to the kitchen to make a pot of coffee. While I was pouring the water through the filter, I thought: well, when this is done, I'll paint my fingernails."

I must have looked surprised, because Sara laughed again. "You have to understand. I'm having an identity crisis. I'm trying to grow them out!" I glanced down. "No," she said, shoving her hands in her pockets. "You have to hear the rest first.

"It must have been Saturday because Eddie was still in bed. Anyway, it hit me all over again that our life together is entirely too marginal. There's no way I can keep up with things. The stairs are always covered with chips trailed in from the woodpile. Just keeping warm is a constant struggle, lugging logs up the stairs, continually shoveling ashes out of the stove, and sweeping up the trail of bark one way and ashes the other. I was feeling like Cinderella, just when somehow I'd decided I wanted to be glamorous." She stopped talking and turned to look at me again. "Does this interest you at all?"

"Absolutely."

"Really? You're not bored? You're not just being polite?"

I smiled. "Sara, my life is rarely boring. You are not boring. Go on."

She cocked her head to the side. "Okay," she said. "Good." And she continued. "I went back down to the woodpile to get one big log, and I grabbed a chunk of oak, and I bent my thumbnail back below the quick. See?" She stuck her hand under my nose with the thumb up. "So much for glamour. I dropped the log and started hopping up and down holding onto my thumb. It really hurt. Finally I went back upstairs and got the tequila and poured myself a straight shot. It was starting to remind me of the year I had strep throat and drank a wasp in my tea! I looked around the room and I thought, I have got to get out of here!" She paused and turned away as if she were looking for something in the trees.

"Very entertaining," I said. She wiped her nose with her cuff, and I knew she was crying.

"Damn," she said, and was quiet for awhile. "I guess I knew all along."

"What?"

"Oh," she looked away again, waving her hand as if to summarize or dismiss what she had been thinking. "Oh, just that it wasn't going to work." She stared off toward the trees where the egrets were nesting, lifted her binoculars and studied the distance. I looked for a moment in the same direction and then back at Sara.

"There's more, why don't you talk about it? You can't see the egrets. I know, I looked before you got here."

She lowered the binoculars. "What is there to say? It's half-hearted, the whole thing. How did I get so involved? How could I have been so stupid?"

She wouldn't look at me. I waited without saying anything, and then I cupped her chin and turned her toward me. I held her a moment before I let go, and we sat facing each other.

"But isn't it stupid to stay when all you do is hurt each other?" She wanted me to tell her. She wanted me to know.

"I can't answer that," I said. "Stupid? I don't think so. You want me to tell you to leave? I've been married for sixteen years, Sara."

"But you do love her. You do love each other."

I shifted my weight on the bench. The wind was cold and blew against my face. "Love is a loaded word," I said.

"What are you talking about?" She turned away again, angrily.

"Give me a break, Sara. This isn't easy."

She fidgeted with her collar and hunched forward on the bench. "I'm sorry," she said. "I shouldn't have come today."

"Why are you saying that? Do you want to hurt me?"

"Maybe I do."

"Sara, Sara." I put my arm around her, and she leaned her head into my chest and cried.

* * *

"I'm not telling anyone anything. They'll have to pry it out of me. I don't have to and I won't. What good would it do me? I don't even know myself what it is I won't tell." Sara never said that, but she could have. I might have heard her say it in a dream. It's not the kind of thing she ever would have said to me, but I think some part of her felt that way. For all the talking she did, there was something she held back, something she could not give.

Sara wanted to know without being known. I thought she wanted to know Eddie as she wished he could know her. But now I wonder if she didn't prefer her privacy, if she didn't want her secrets more. She always had a hidden life. That was her protection. To know, but remain unknown. I must have frightened her. The day when she did not come and I waited alone at the bird sanctuary, an egret circled high above where I sat, its wings folding the wind over and over as it rose steadily higher, and at some point I knew quite certainly that Sara would never come, not that day or ever again.

At first, in a panic that kept my understanding at a distance, I thought she was dead, and in a way she was. I had seen her for the last time, when she sat beside me on the bench in the fog, training her binoculars on the place where the nests were hidden, pretending to see them. Pretending so she could hide her feelings from me.

When I stopped for gas on the way home that day, the same attendant was wearing the black shirt with his annoucement: FIGHT CRIME shoot back. I felt I had come full circle when I returned to the road, which was strangely empty. To the north I saw a pair of mallards drop down to the surface of the marsh where they landed on the silver water near a clump of reeds, and I felt something soften in me, something let go.

The flowering quince beside our mailbox seemed to have bloomed overnight, and as I drove up to the house, I saw Elaine through the window. She was sitting at the piano, swaying slightly as she played. She had her eyes closed, and when she leaned her head back, her dark hair fell away from her neck, leaving the curve of her throat exposed. She must have heard the car door slam, for when I glanced again at the window as I walked up the steps, she had straightened and collected herself, though she must have known it was only me coming home.

*   *   *

Our house is not at all like the house Elaine grew up in, the old house, as she calls it. That house was bigger and darker, though perhaps it was really the eastern climate and those long winters which made it seem darker. The house we live in is filled with sunlight. The windows are large and the walls are white. There is one doorway unlike any other in the house, a high arched doorway. I think absently about that particular doorway, about the way it sweeps up and under the wall and down again, unlike any of the other doorways which are squared off, rigidly separating one room from another.

The arched doorway has no door. Placed between the living room and hallway, there is something inviting about its opening. The arch reminds me of the back of a cat lifting up under your hand when you stroke it. It says something about pleasure, about invitations.

From my study I see Elaine in the living room, leaning against the opposite wall, her own back pressed against the cool plaster. Afternoon sun casts a swath of light on the oak floor. I imagine she lets her eyes swim across the boards, lets the grain in the shadowed places slowly blur, shifts her gaze to the sunny place and back to the shadow, letting the blindness of sudden contrast temporarily obliterate everything.

The doorway with the arch, opening into the dim hall, a hall that leads to other rooms, reminds me of last night, of standing in it, leaning against one side, the way she leans now into the opposite wall, of watching her, my hand wrapped around a can of beer.

Sunlight licks her bare feet and she straightens. The kids will be home soon. Maybe she thinks she should get something out of the freezer for dinner or fold the laundry, but she doesn't move. She stands in the sun, dreamily looking through the high arched opening.

She remembers leaning toward him, her husband reaching for her, humming an old song—*only you can make my life complete*—the slow dance they did under that arch till he guided her into the hallway. "Shh," she warned him not to wake the kids, his hum lowering to a vibration as he laughed, his laughter caught there in his throat, like another kind of music she thought. His arm across her shoulders, the cold aluminum can against her skin.

Her husband. I took her in my arms and slow danced her across the living room.

"Welcome home," she said, drawing away from me, smiling that smile that always seems a little like there's a joke I'm not getting. "It's been a while."

"What?" I murmured.

"Never mind. Is the story finished?"

"Yes."

"I missed you. It's nice to have you back."

"I haven't been anywhere."

"No?" She sighed, and I pulled her close again as I danced her into the hall.

☙

PHOTO BY B. J. FUNDARO

Elizabeth Herron published her first collection of poems, *Desire Being Full of Distances* (Calliopea Press), in 1983. In 1986 her cassette, "Inside the World," came out. *While the Distance Widens* is her first collection of short fiction. She teaches at Sonoma State University in the Arts & Humanities Mentor Program, where she also is Faculty Advisor to the University's magazine, *Sonoma Mandala Literary Review.* Herron is known for her performance of sung and chanted poetry. She lives in western Sonoma County.

COLOPHON

One thousand copies of *While the Distance Widens*
were printed and bound in Ann Arbor, Michigan
by McNaughton & Gunn, Inc., in the fall of 1992.
Designed and produced at Archetype West by
Michael Sykes. The type for the text is Baskerville,
with the titles of the stories in Optima. The cover
painting is by Elizabeth Herron.

Selected Titles from Floating Island Publications

Up My Coast by Joanne Kyger
5 ½ x 8 ½ / 24 pp / $5.00

Dazzled by Arthur Sze
5 ½ x 9 ¼ / 60 pp / $8.00

Two Weeks Off by Kirk Robertson
6 x 9 / 32 pp / $5.00

Black Ash, Orange Fire by William Witherup
6 x 9 / 224 pp / $12.00

Flying the Red Eye by Frank Stewart
6 x 9 / 56 pp / $8.00

Point Reyes Poems by Robert Bly
5 ½ x 7 / 32 pp / $6.00

Ordinary Messengers by Michael Hannon
6 x 8 / 88 pp / $10.00

Seminary Poems by Diane di Prima
5 ½ x 7 / 48 pp / $6.00

Park by Cole Swensen
5 ½ x 7 / 64 pp / $8.00

The Raven Wakes Me Up by Stephan Torre
6 x 9 / 48 pp / $8.00

Blue Skies by Robert Fromberg
5 ½ x 7 / 48 pp / $6.00

Ten Poems By Issa by Robert Bly
5 ½ x 7 / 32 pp / $6.00

No Film in the Camera by Nancy Lay
5 ½ x 8 ½ / 64 pp / $8.00